# Rose City Ink

Presents...

# Beyond A Broken Dream 2

### New Dreams

Written by,

*Sondra N*

All rights reserved. No part of this book may be reproduced in any form or by any means without prior written consent from the Publisher, except brief quotes used for reviews.

Any and all persons or situations contained in this book came from the imagination of the Author or are used fictitiously, so any similarities are coincidental.

Visit me on Facebook:

Printed in the USA

Publisher: Rose City Ink

Cover Designer: Vassie Thompson Jr.

Editor: Shelli Marie/Teruka B

Final Edit: Sondra N

Copyright © 2015 Sondra N

## ACKNOWLEDGEMENTS

I have got to give huge props and respect to Vassie Thompson Jr. Your cover work is fantastic, can't tell a book by its cover, but your covers sure bring the interest.

Thank you to CamRon Bell, for helping me to do things on the Word program that need done. You are always ready and willing to help, and I appreciate that.

Thank you Nicollette Nettles for proof reading, helping me edit and pointing out all the mistakes you can find! I love you for that and so many other reasons, always. And yes, every book I write is coming your way.

Thank you for the people that actually read my first book, and for those reading this one as well. I appreciate you beyond words. Thank you for those that did reviews for me and shun the light in such a positive manner.

And thank you a million times over for those that messaged me advice, and pointers on editing, to help me to write better and deliver a better finished story.

Special thanks to Shelli Marie's Rose City Readers. I love my Facebook groups, and this group is nothing but positive love, lifting the spirit, sharing good reads and full of support.

The ladies at Rose City Ink.

Shelli Marie and Teruka B...I promise you any day you contact me I need something. Thank you for all of your help to make this possible, and to help me learn along the way. You ladies are on it, much respect. Know that I am on the team, and so grateful to be a part of.

## DEDICATION

This book is dedicated to the victims of Hurricane Katrina.

To the ones that did not survive.

To the ones unable to return home.

To the ones still lost.

And lastly to the ones that carry the wounds and strive for the healing.

Dreams can and do come true, and the fact that you are reading my book proves it, I hope you will continue to do so and hope you will enjoy each one even more.

CELESTE'S STORY

# Recap from Beyond a broken dream, Celeste's story book 1:

    She checked her phone and saw Halle had called her, when she listened to the voice mail it was not sounding good. Her friend was no doubt coking and drinking and Celeste was sure she was not alone.

    This did not help her almost sleepless night.

    In the morning while she drank her coffee she listened again to voicemails and heard Halle leaving a message that she was at Celeste's hotel door. It had been 5 A.M. And Celeste knew she had made the right move by leaving there. 'Damn it!' She considered dumping her phone and getting a new one once she got out of the area. Getting out of the area could not come quick enough.

When Celeste started loading the rental car she noticed a car in the parking lot that had at least three men in it. The windows were tinted but she could feel them looking at her.

When she pulled out of the hotel lot she saw that car getting ready to pull out too and as she drove to the Cadillac dealership she kept looking in her rearview for the car but was unable to see it. She hoped it had been a coincidence and had nothing to do with her.

She parked her little rental on the side street. Walking in Celeste asked for the manager and told him she wanted to buy the pearl white Deville with cash and wanted to give him a bonus for his trouble.

In his private office she gave him fifty thousand dollars and let him worry about the paperwork. Giving him enough information and signing enough documents to complete the deal. While he was out of the room she called her insurance, added the car on and was driving away within the hour.

Celeste was ready to hit the road on her way out of town with what was now new dreams becoming a new reality she had not even imagined.

She pulled up behind the rental car. She popped the trunk and got out of her new car going to the rental and opening that trunk and door, leaving the keys under the floor mat so the rental agency could pick up their car.

As she went to get out her luggage and transfer from the rental car to her new ride she saw that damn car again, coming down the street toward her, slowing and pulling right up next to her. Celeste knew no way could she get away before their car doors opened.

# Beyond A Broke Dream 2
# New Dreams

# Chapter 1

    Pure terror covered Celeste's whole being as she saw the car door ready to open. She didn't know what to do when she saw the police car pull right up behind her with their sirens blaring and the lights flashing.

    She slammed the trunk of her car down, hardly able to breathe. The two cops got out and approached both sides of the vehicle next to her. Taking a deep breath, Celeste got into her brand new car trying not to look as scared as she felt.

    Uncertain if she would also be detained, but she felt such relief when one of the officers waved her to back up. He then gave an arm signal letting her know she could go around and Celeste did so gladly.

Every part of her body trembled from the inside out, she wanted to get a good look of who was in the car next to her, but she was too scared. Celeste took a quick glance but she did not recognize any of the men.

'What the hell? Who were these guys and why did they follow her and wait for her? 'Maybe they know that I have money, or have connected me with Halle,' she thought.

Thank God they were being detained; Celeste hoped they were riding dirty and really detained for a long time. She also hoped to hell her name and anything about her stayed out of their mouths.

Celeste quickly and carefully followed the directions to get the hell out of Alexandria. Celeste took I-495 toward Richmond, merging onto I-66 West.

She drove on the I-66 for about an hour, feeling assured she was not followed and safely on her way as she merged onto the I-81 South. The more freeways she entered on, the more miles she traveled away from Alexandria Virginia, away from Washington D.C., the better she felt. There were about 375 miles to Knoxville, and she felt safe to stop for the restroom.

Celeste stopped by a Mom & Pops convenient store to gas up. Once inside, she grabbed a sandwich, Cherry slushy and bottled water. She figured that she would make it to Knoxville by seven that evening, have dinner there and she would call in a day.

She got back into her car and said a prayer. It was a prayer of thanks and a prayer for Halle.

What a total relief to be out of the D.C. area. Images of the night before burned into her mind. It was such a horror to witness, and there was such fear surrounding this huge score that happened in her and Halle's life. Then after knowing she was being hunted this morning, there was fresh terror that ran through her body. She was afraid for Halle... really afraid. Something was not right.

Celeste had her phone volume turned off, and the voicemail was letting callers know she was no longer in the area and would not be returning calls. Every so often she heard a ding which meant another voicemail had been left.

Celeste figured on her next stop she would listen to her voicemails, and call Halle rather than waiting for her to leave another message. Celeste knew Halle was either crashed out or even worse; still awake and flying high.

Taking a moment to reflect on her own past drug use. She was now in her fourteenth year of being clean. Celeste was in total bliss, and her gratitude reached to the highest of mountains, and she made sure to start her prayers every night with this gratitude. If she had still been using she too would have shared in the drugs and God only knew where she would be today. She knew for a fact that she would not have four-hundred fifty thousand, a brand new luxury car and be on the road a free woman with a life of possibilities before her.

As the miles and the minutes flew by Celeste relaxed, feeling like she had got away and was able to begin to actually enjoy the ride. This brand new pearly white Deville was smooth. She loved every minute of it. Summer was on and humid, but this new ride was, smooth, comfortable. She loved it, often driving with the window open just feeling the warm air.

The scenery was lovely too. Company would be nice to enjoy the sights with, but Celeste was not feeling lonely. She had certainly learned to appreciate her own company and actually enjoyed the time alone to process the sudden changes that had happened to her.

Celeste dug in her bag and retrieved one of her Luther Vandross CD's out and popped it into the CD player. She sang along with the songs while riding through Virginia, loving the scenery and the drive.

Celeste was trying to block out the images of a man dying in front of her from the night before. And also attempting to block the images her own mind was creating when thinking of Halle and where and how she was.

She stopped again after crossing into Tennessee a few hours later, her bladder was beyond full. Celeste stretched, took long strides with her legs, and lunged a few times. She filled up the tank, emptied trash.

Celeste went in and bought snacks, including something sweet and a large black coffee and another water refill. It was nice just to talk a little with people and stretch her legs.

She played and deleted a multitude of voicemails and realized Halle had not left her another one. *'Okay, that probably meant she had crashed and that was a good sign,'* she thought. Celeste called Halle and the phone took her straight to voicemail, which was full so Celeste could not even leave her a message. "Damn it!" She said out loud. Having voicemail and not using it was an irritant and in this case it gave her an eerie feeling but she hoped there was some kind of logical reason for it. Somehow though, deep in her heart, she felt that something terrible had happened.

Only another two hours and she would be in Knoxville, so she drank the coffee and ate a candy bar with the window open to wake her ass up some more. She switched up her CD to Dwight Yoakum. She could get her groove on with his sexy country twang.

Celeste got onto the I-40, a half hour away from her room for the night. She had booked at The Fairfield Inn and Suites. It sat right next to a Cracker Barrel Old Country Store, which was actually on Cracker Barrel Lane. She already knew that was a good sign and had to be a full win situation.

Once checked into the hotel she turned on the computer and made a pot of coffee. Celeste did news searches for Washington D.C., seeing nothing of interest. It was Sunday evening and she fully expected there to be something in the news about George by the next day.

Changing into her bathing suit, she took a swim and had a short hot tub session. Back up in her room she indulged in a long shampoo and shower. Feeling very refreshed, she dried off with a fluffy towel, creamed lotion on her body, and slipped into a maxi dress. Celeste then walked over to The Cracker Barrel to enjoy a Sunday chicken dinner. She loved everything about The Cracker Barrel. These restaurants were not located anywhere near her hometown, so she made sure to indulge every chance she got.

    She loved the home cooking, good portions, with great prices, you can't beat that. She totally dug the antiques all over the walls to look at, and the big stone fireplace that was in each dining room. Upon leaving, there was the Country Store that had old style candies and treasures that begged to be browsed through. It was a re-visit to childhood, and uplifting.

    "Thank goodness I got folks back home to justify some gifts," she laughed with the lady bagging her goodies which included a wonderful body spray with pearls in the bottle for herself.

    The walk back to the hotel was pleasant. The area felt good. Once back to the room Celeste got on the computer again, checking out her next day's travels and played some games to pass the time and unwind.

    Finally she shut down and lay naked with the window open and got totally into her book "Standing on the Scratch Line" written by Guy Johnson, Maya Angelou's son. Reading until her eye lids were too heavy to stay open, she slept very deep. A good kind of tired and a great kind of comfortable...

# Chapter 2

The next morning Celeste got down with blueberry pancakes and bacon with black coffee at the Cracker Barrel. It was a damn good breakfast.

She checked voicemails again; damn, these D.C. dudes just kept calling and leaving messages. Her voicemail message told callers she was not in the area and not returning calls. Obviously that was not stopping the repeat calls and messages. It was a weary process going through and deleting all of those messages, but it had to be done.

Looking over map directions for the day, there was about twenty miles on the I-40, and then getting over on the I-75 going about eighty three miles, cross into Georgia and then one hundred twenty three miles into Alabama. After that, there would be thirty three miles to Birmingham and another three hours to Meridian Mississippi. That was where she had made a reservation at a Hilton Garden Inn and what her goal for the day was. Something about staying in Birmingham didn't excite her, but she figured it could be a good dinner stop if nothing else.

Celeste checked out of the hotel paying cash, made sure she hit an ATM to make a cash deposit too, before getting back on the freeway.

The day was hot and the drive was draining her. So much time in the car...She made frequent stops to walk, use the restroom, stay hydrated and snack her way through the states. It was a long day and she was glad to have a short trip to New Orleans the next day. Then there would be several days of rest before heading across the country to Oregon. She didn't even want to think about that journey on her own. In Meridian Mississippi when she got to the room, the A.C. was kickin' and Celeste slipped her shoes off and lay on the bed. She put the TV on and just chilled for a while.

Finally dragging herself off the bed, she powered up the computer and got it going. She checked the news in D.C. and was shocked at what she saw. George William Weatherall had been discovered that morning in his Georgetown home dead, in what the news was reporting looked like natural causes.

Now she knew his full name, and that he was a member of Congress and had been set to testify that week at a Congressional Hearing. That was the man she and Halle had seen and watched die. Halle and Celeste had also helped themselves to a million dollars that rested in his closet.

The news also stated that there was no suspicion; the whole thing seemed downplayed, but she let it go.  That was what was shocking. There was his government history mentioned and that he would be missed and so on, and it felt to Celeste like a cover up already in play.

The huge amount of cocaine she and Halle had seen him doing had her wondering what else was in his home. The large amount of cash not being mentioned made sense. Who would know a million dollars had been in a closet and was now gone?

It just felt like there was more that should have been stumbled on. Halle had used zip locks to take the coke, but surely there was some kind of remains left there. The ice bucket had been overflowing with cocaine.  Certainly from what Celeste had seen, that did not look like no kind of natural causes to her. A part of her was relieved. Another part that was very leery.

Halle's phone was still going straight to voicemail and her mailbox still full. *'Not even cool,'* she thought. Celeste checked ads and saw that Halle had not posted, but then again why in the world would she with the windfall Celeste hoped she still had. Again she had a bad feeling, and knew there was not a damn thing she could do about it.

"Damn it!" she shouted. Celeste wished this girl would try to call her again or would clear her messages, something.

Celeste called her daughter Valerie, back in Oregon just to check in and update her. "Hey baby! I got a new plan on getting home. I'm not going to be flying."

"How is that Mama? What's going on?" Valerie inquired.

"Baby, I met a guy fully loaded! He bought me a brand new Cadillac," she lied. "I'm taking a road trip back home. I'm going to see your Aunt Yvette for a few days in New Orleans. I get there tomorrow."

"What? Wow! D.C was good to you. You driving alone?" Valerie sounded a little worried.

"Yeah but I'm good, taking it easy, resting on the way. I'll let you know when I leave New Orleans and keep you posted," Celeste calmly explained to her daughter hoping to reassure her.

"Yes, please do that. Tell Auntie Yvette hello from me."

After disconnecting the call, Celeste called Yvette, and her sister was delighted to hear she would be arriving the next day. Her place was only a two bedroom 'small apartment above her store in the Quarter, but she assured Celeste there was room and she was welcome.

Once she finished, Celeste started doing random searches for drug overdoses. Searching for any bodies found or arrests made in the Alexandria Virginia area. She found nothing that fit Halle and so was hopeful things were alright with her friend. Really, it was not totally out of character for Halle to go missing like that. She had done so on other occasions.

Halle in the past had checked herself in a nice hotel with room service, did not work, and just used and hung there until her money was gone. Celeste tried to feel reassured that Halle was just doing her and things were okay. Halle had been on the streets and cross country fending for her own self since she was a teenager, so certainly now that she had a whole lot of cash maybe she was just figuring out her game plan and doing some "Her" time.

Hell, she might even be laid up with that square she had been so sprung on. Her mind was feeling crazy with scenarios going through her head. Celeste was straight up worried about her girl and feeling pissed too, out of fear and worry!

After taking a refreshing shower and lathering lotion all over her body, she was surprised how much sun she had taken in and saw her left arm darker than the right.

*'Like a darn truck driver,'* she thought. More sun screen needed tomorrow for sure…

# Chapter 3

The next morning having coffee in her room, Celeste felt very excited about getting to New Orleans that day. It was only about three hours and then she would not have to get in the car again for a while. She was so glad to be able to see Yvette and tell her what had happened, to be able to talk about it and also get her opinion and advice. Yvette was very good with finances and had done quite well for herself, so she knew that she could use her help.

Her sister had married well, and enjoyed a life of privilege and luxury. Her cheating husband, however, had been missing for four years. He had taken a trip to Hong Kong and had not been seen or heard from since. Three more years and everything in his name would go to Yvette.

They had two grown children in Ivy League Colleges and Yvette was doing the single life in a vibrant city full of history and possibilities. An avid reader, she had bought a book store that had become a metaphysical shop. Those days, what books were in the shop contained information about the city, Voodoo, candle magic, healing crystals and inner peace. Her apartment was above the shop. Celeste had not seen the set up yet but she and her sister shared many letters keeping up on their life's events.

Celeste had a buffet style breakfast at the hotel in Mississippi. Once in the car, a pillowcase was under her butt since she had elected to wear shorts. After gassing up and making her cash deposit in an ATM, with her mocha and bottled water in hand, she headed out. I-59 was a straight shot. New Orleans was only a few hours away.

Anytime Celeste saw an ATM of her bank that accepted deposits she stopped and dropped a grand or so in her account.

At check-out, she paid her hotel bills in cash.  Knowing a few hours from now a bulk of her money would be put into her sisters' safe and feeling glad about that. Celeste did not enjoy driving solo with this much cash on her. The drive had been pretty attention to herself or uneventful, partially due to the fact that she was not calling involving herself in any kind of sketchy situations. Sometimes bad things did randomly happen to people, but a whole lot of times people made choices that found themselves in situations where it was more likely. She chose to be the former.

Having checked the computer for updates from the D.C. area, she had only found more of the same on George William Weatherall. She couldn't help but feel like there were those better off with him dead and not being able to testify.

Money was power and power was money and she knew this was a big game in politics. She expected that it was only what those in charge wanted released. They just tell the public some information in the way they wanted it done. Celeste knew this, but what she did not know was what was really going on behind the scenes.

'Would it all be swept under the rug? Hushed and closed? Or were there any high powered dangerous people looking for cash and answers?' She did not know and did not want to find out.

Celeste was pretty sure that the car of men that had pulled next to her in Alexandria Virginia and were then held up by the police had nothing to do with George William Weatherall. Instead she felt somehow they had come and followed her because of Halle and she feared for Halle.

There were comments though that the testimony of George William Weatherall was to have been vital to proceedings and it had to do with energy. It looked like some big business oil money would not mourn his passing. Celeste was a little surprised there was no cocaine angle brought into the news. Scandals and cover-ups were not just for TV and books, real life mimicked for real.

*****

It was such a pleasure to enter into New Orleans and drive over to her sister's place. Celeste parked a little ways up from the shop, grabbed a couple of her bags and headed upstairs. Yvette swung the door open and gave her a huge embrace.

"Hi Celeste! Look at you. Man Sis, you got some sun. You look good," she giggled.

Yvette was absolutely gorgeous, a natural shade darker than Celeste, ocean green eyes and a rich red to her hair that just brightened her up.

Never could her sister go anywhere and not be noticed.

She was so toned, always into fitness and exercise; it was a part of her daily life. She had long legs and was a natural busty double D. The girl wore a bra to bed all of her life, while Celeste had ran around through the seventies au natural, braless and free. The difference may have always existed anyway but Celeste knew Yvette worked at keeping herself in prime. She had a sexy gypsy appeal. Her bracelets snaked up one arm, beads everywhere, wild hair and confidence. Celeste was sure when she was in her shop she would look like a Voodoo priestess to many.

"Yvette!! Girl I am so glad to see you, you don't even know! My God you look fantastic. I love you in New Orleans!"

Yvette laughed, her sisters' loud enthusiasm catching, and they walked together back to Celeste's car. She helped get bags into her apartment, complimenting Celeste on her new ride as they walked.

"Okay, this car is bad assed, you have seriously got a whole lot of story to tell me."

"You don't even know! There is so much I need to let you know. I have not been able to tell anybody, and I have spent way too much time alone these last days in the car and in hotel rooms. I really need to talk about a lot Sis," Celeste agreed.

"That's why I'm not working today. Let's go do lunch and you can let me know everything!"

"Yvette, you know what I really got a taste for? A muffuletta sandwich. That New Orleans classic is what I am craving. You know a place we can walk to?"

"Of course, but honey let's drive this car up a few blocks to a lot and go from there."

The sounds and sights were so wonderful, a comfort really. This was a city Celeste knew she would always love and 'Oh My Gosh', the food, it was mouthwatering. That sandwich was satisfying with the olive salad spread on the perfect muffuletta bread and cold cuts. It was on point and Celeste dug in as Yvette enjoyed a po' boy southern style.

While they grubbed up, Celeste filled her in on what had happened in D.C. and how it had all come down. Yvette had some questions on what she did afterwards and who she had talked to about what she knew. She seemed relieved to hear. Celeste kept her mouth shut and moved quickly getting out of the area.

"Man Celeste. Your friend...all that doesn't sound too good, but I'm so glad you left. I don't view it like you did anything wrong. A situation arose and you acted on the best option. That George guy was up to no good, you can bet that. Nobody has a million bucks in their closet that isn't up to something shady. So now, what are you going to do with this money to get yourself secured?"

"Well Sis, what I want to do is buy a house in Oregon. I mean... all my kids and grandbabies are so that is home for me. But yeah, I would love to get out of my apartment. I have been doing my taxes, but I don't think I can get approved getting into a house," I continued. "How would you feel about me giving you cash and you purchase out right? I know you got the funds and paperwork to go with it. What I would love and what I was thinking is like put $300,000.00 wherever you can put it... buy a house and keep a kick back for yourself as a gift for your troubles?" Celeste looked at her hopefully.

"Sure, I can do that. You don't have to throw money at me though, I would rather you put some in investments," Yvette spoke in a serious tone.

"Well, I plan to put $100,000.00 in a mutual funds market account. I got to slip it into my bank in segments though. I can't do anything over

$10,000 at a time. I figure I can get a home in the $250,000.00 range free and clear, live off the other $50,000 and be in a pretty set stich. Giving you $50,000 as well and please don't even start trippin' about it. Everybody can use more money; you can splurge even, since it is an unexpected gift. You know, good fortune needs shared."

"Okay Celeste, well I can help you with investments and I got a safe, we need to go get some of this money into. It makes me nervous, you driving across country with that kind of cash by yourself. Now tell me why the hell my brother in law married that damn no account female instead of continuing his life with you?"

"Yvette I don't know. I really don't. There kept being indications, you know, and a part of me wanted so badly for him to pursue me. Woo me, do it right and all that. I don't know if he felt guilty about leading her on. I don't know if the bitch used some bad mojo or what, but I know without any kind of doubt how deeply he loves me. He actually told me he was not *'in love'* with her, but apparently he aint *'in love'* with me either. It hurt so fucking bad till I just had to leave town. I can't even stand thinking about him and her being together when I lay down at night and again when I wake in the morning."

Celeste sighed, let out a deep breath and then got real on another level. "I think I need a little help from something at your shop to get things right. What I feel like, truth be told is some damn revenge, and I really am having some evil assed thoughts about her."

Yvette gave her Sister an appraising look. "You know what honey? You will be happier when you forgive. I promise you. And yeah, I be wanting to do something to get even. Wanting to hurt back is normal."

Yvette placed her hand on Celeste's and continued, "The thing is, it is him that did you wrong.

"She could be any of the she's out there. If it wasn't her it would be another, and let me tell you something," Yvette spoke looking directly into her sister's eyes and went on. "What she has aint nothing you have not already had and you already know how it goes. The man was with you and had her on the side; he will now be with her and others on the side too. A leopard don't change its spots honey, there is nothing you need to do, just sit back and enjoy the show. It has already been done, it is already in progress." Yvette took a breath and then let her sister know.

"Now for you, for yourself, you put his picture backwards in your wallet and we'll look at some other things to help you. You have to realize you are all you can help. You can't change what he has chosen, so help yourself. Now, that is something I can help you with. Don't you know honey, the very best revenge is a life well lived?"

"I love you so much Yvette, God, thank you. Thank you for letting me be imperfect and loving me anyway, and yes, I will accept help and words of wisdom. Celeste gave her a hug as they exited the restaurant and headed back to Yvette's spot on Conti near Burgundy Street.

Yvette was talking history along the way, pointing out what had once been Ernest J Bellocq's home. He was a well-known photographer of the ladies of Storyville. Storyville was an area where prostitution was allowed and contained in the early 1900s. The home actually was a place of prostitution later as well, used by Norma Wallace who was quite the character well into the 1970s.

Celeste laughed out loud. "Girl I love this kind of history. To think back to school days I thought history was boring. This true life stuff is fascinating for real."

Money in the safe, Celeste started a load of clothes and got settled into Yvette's spare bedroom.

Her furnishings were elegant and very tasteful. She really dug the vibe and the stories Yvette shared about the home's history. Yvette told her like so many places in the quarter her shop stayed open late, until 10 P.M., and opened 10 A.M. She had a few local gals that enjoyed sitting shop. They didn't mind doing a shift and especially liked the discount they received on items. Really, it was a hobby for Yvette more than an income. If the shop made the lease payment each month which included her apartment, then it was all good. She felt that whenever she decided to move it could be a good rental in the coming years.

For now Yvette enjoyed not having to worry about a big home and a big yard. She had done the mansion thing when her husband was with her and raising the kids. Her kids had always had such busy schedules, and that meant that Yvette did as well. Driving was a part of her *'stay at home'* mom description. As well as charity involvements, opera, board meetings, and doing without her husband far more than she did with him. So this quieter smaller life right now suited her and she planned to stay another few years while the kids finished school and her husband had been missing long enough to make it final.

    Celeste had never asked Yvette what she thought happened to her husband. She was pretty sure he was dead, but rather or not her sister had more information Celeste was not certain. Her brother-in-law went to Hong Kong as he often had done and never came back or was heard from. Contacts were made, dead ends were reached and Celeste looked at Yvette thinking, *'She does not look grief stricken, nor worried. Matter of fact she seemed far less stiff and uptight than I have seen her in years.'* A strained marriage has a way of affecting a woman. The tension, worry, and disappointments will take its toll. Well, it looked like Yvette had figured out how to let it go in the Big Easy.

# Chapter 4

Their visit was cut short when Yvette let Celeste know that she needed to step out for a few. Celeste was let down a little bit, because she expected to spend the entire day chatting with her sister.

Before leaving out Yvette scheduled Celeste a massage at the local spa. She figured since Celeste had taken that long drive, her body could use a bit of relaxation.

Celeste lay naked on a massage table; lights dimmed, covered with a sheet and let her body relax to the deep tissue work the masseuse was giving her. She thought about her sister. She loved her deeply but knew Yvette had always been a rather private person and her depth was far more than reached the eye. Celeste had learned long ago not to question and not to pry. Yvette would share what she wanted and when she wanted. Celeste was far more open by nature. She was thankful though that never once, no matter what it had ever been, had she felt Yvette judged, condemned or looked down on her. She knew she could trust her completely.

After the massage Celeste's entire body felt heavy and walking back through the active streets she was so glad to be there. New Orleans was like another country in many ways. Old ways, old styles, an eclectic mix that she loved. It was not long of a walk without walking by a cool little spot to groove in, an interesting shop to browse in. Since she needed to drink a large amount of water after her massage, she decided to stop into one little spot and drink an ice cold water while she waited for a wonderful icy blended non-alcoholic drink to take with her. Her drink was served in the traditional plastic cup that all drinks got served in so she walked out with it, already feeling much more hydrated and better. Once she got to her sisters shop she went through the door.

Wow, there were things of interest everywhere. Crystals and medicinal herbs lined the shelves. Potions and lotions were everywhere.

Gris Gris, candles and Hoodoo dolls caught her eye. She knew that a lot of people thought these were to bring harm, but they were actually to bless. There were amulets to protect from evil, and some to bring the wearer luck. Items for ones shrine, their work station or alter. There were cauldrons even to burn herbs in. She felt drawn to many items. So much was appealing to her and she enjoyed browsing.

There was so very much misunderstanding of spiritual practices and beliefs as being evil and wrong. There were many religions much older than Christianity, and even that popular religion had been changed up by Kings Translation and there was so much elimination in the infamous book, called the Bible.

Celeste personally was very accepting and even embraced other world views, there were so many. Being an American really could limit the world view and make one's mind only open on a small scale.

She browsed some books, and saw a picture of Marie Laveau's tomb, in the oldest cemetery in New Orleans.

At the time Marie Laveau lived in the city, there were fifteen well known Voodoo Queens, although she was known as the most powerful. She had also been a Catholic and encouraged and influenced a great many to worship and attend the Catholic Church. Because Marie was a hairdresser, she knew all the gossip in town. This amused Celeste, 'Some things really never changed,' she thought.

Ms. Laveau was well known and loved, and still to this day honored and remembered fondly. She was said to have been a caring and compassionate woman. She had died in 1881 and her powerful ways are said to have helped many. Including finding slaves their freedom. Those both white and of color that were in political positions also sought her help out.

An elderly woman entered the shop with a bundle of something in newsprint. She was very dark and seemed to walk slowly and carefully. The lady that was present in the shop greeted her warmly and with respect "Bienvenue Chere Madame."(In English this meant welcome dear madam in literal translation.)

The woman returned a smile and greeting, "Bonjure mon cher." (hello my dear). She kept walking straight up to Celeste, handing her the bundle and telling her first in French and then in English "to take it upstairs now," she spoke with a very pronounced accent. Celeste heard what a

Haitian accent was most likely, and thanked her in French. She could at least manage that.

"Merci de bien vouloir Madame." When she reached for the bundle she felt a sense of well-being and as instructed took it upstairs.

Yvette greeted her, in the process of setting her small table for two.

"Ahh, you saw Nathaima. You can set that on the counter for later."

"That is a beautiful name. I was not introduced but she walked right to me, she has great energy," Celeste responded and went to wash her hands.

"That she does indeed. I saw her out earlier and she said she would be in the area to drop some herbs by. You can put those on the counter for later. I made Caesar salad, grilled shrimp and bread. We can watch a movie during dinner if you would like. I got *'Feast of All Saints.'*"

"Yvette, Yes. Dinner sounds perfect, and so does the movie. It is one of my favorites," Celeste replied as she began to fill her plate. "That is a movie that is done so very well. Most of the time I like the book so much better, but in this case they are both excellent and it's a perfect choice, so very

Nawlins!" She said in excitement referring to New Orleans.

Yvette laughed, "Our beloved Anne Rice would be delighted to hear that. Have you seen her home over in the Garden District?"

"I have. That is such a great neighborhood. I bet she doesn't really dig it on tour though. I guess it is part of fame. You know out walking, all the iron lace, the old feel of this area, the Creole influence... I really love this place. I'm so glad to be here."

Yvette let her know she was glad too and the sisters sat to enjoy dinner and a movie.

*****

The next morning Celeste woke to the wonderful smell of strong black coffee and noticed her sister had used some chicory. There was also a plate of beignets with powder sugar sitting next to the pot. For real New Orleans treats. There was a note left that said Yvette would be downstairs, she had some stock to take care of.

Celeste normally did not eat first thing in the morning, so she poured a mug of the delicious coffee and stepped on the balcony to enjoy, with a cigarette before throwing on a dress and heading downstairs.

"Good morning Yvette. What a nice wake up chere thank you," Celeste greeted her Sister.

"Mornin Chere yourself," Yvette laughed. "You got the local flava coming to you and coming from you."

"Guilty. I'm in the zone. You want some help?" Celeste asked. "I would love to help anyway I can, I dig everything in here and it would be a pleasure."

"Okay, there are herbs to put into jars and a few oddities to shelf. Jump in if you want." Yvette gestured to some boxes next to her.

The girls got these tasks done and talked about plans for the day. They were going to head out to Lake Pontchartrain and take the causeway, (the bridge sitting on water the twenty three miles over to the North Shore) to Mandeville. They were going over to see some second cousins.

Big Mama had raised their mother after her own mama had been killed. She would not even have it if Celeste was anywhere in the state and did not come out and have a fish fry and say hello.

They pulled up onto the crushed oyster shell driveway and parked off to the side. First thing Celeste saw was Big Mama. She ran into her arms and they embraced. Then Big Mama took hold of her hand and took her in the kitchen to give her a praline lesson and told her not to leave without taking a container full.

Celeste loved the Spanish moss on the trees in the yard and the creek that ran alongside the property. It felt like home to her heart even though she herself had never lived there. The energy was very good, and when people hollered out... 'Laissez les bon temps roulez!' she joined in too...(let the good times roll!) It was shouted with a joy of living and the meaning was deep in its simple French words.

The get together turned out to be a total blast. The catfish fried up, a table full of sides and Zydeco playing. The atmosphere was a party for sure. Some moves were taught by these Creoles and Cajuns that made a party happen out in the big yard. Celeste and Yvette both had a total blast, and Yvette was much more versed on who was family and how far out the lines went.

Celeste had her eye on a fine assed Creole man, and hoped to learn he was not kin and also hoped to see him again. She pulled Yvette over and got a proper introduction to this gorgeous man who was absolutely of no relation.

"Laurent Amonester, I would like to introduce my sister, Miss Celeste Lacoste," Yvette said using their Mother's birth name.

When he replied it sounded like music. He took Celeste's hand in his brushed it with his lips, and looked into her eyes as he responded, "C'est unplaisir de vous rencontrer." Celeste did not know much French but knew he had said it was a pleasure to meet her and she replied in English, "The pleasure is all mine."

She allowed herself to be held in his arms while they danced, and was seduced by his velvety voice and smooth way of delivering. The man was fine, everything about him appealed to her and they exchanged numbers before she and Yvette headed back to New Orleans. Celeste felt her body respond and wetness in her panties she had not felt in a very long time. Cherishing the fantasy, she considered making love with this man before she left the area completely.

She had noticed that he hadn't had a bottle of beer, nor a mixed drink. In her mind this was a huge plus. An alcohol fueled conversation was not her cup of tea; she liked a sober man saying what he felt and what he meant, with real courage, not needing the false courage of alcohol. This had strong appeal to her and her interest had grown throughout the afternoon and into the evening.

She mentioned her interest in Laurent to her sister to get some feedback and Yvette laughed in delight.

"Girl, he is fine and a real sweetheart. His wife died a year ago; I don't think he has seen anybody since. You know he got a place in Metairie?" she explained.

"Yeah he mentioned that, we exchanged numbers. I'm thinking of having an evening with him tomorrow," Celeste admitted. As she spoke the words she realized indeed, she was looking forward to it.

"That's cool, but I got to let you know your travel day should be Friday morning. I did some inquiring and that is your best day to begin your journey home....course if you do plan to stay longer, I can research and find another," Yvette spoke up letting her know.

"No, Friday is cool. I got a long drive. Anything else you want to share with me sister?" Celeste looked at Yvette's profile as she drove over the bridge, sensing she knew something and Celeste was eager for information.

"Celeste, the dead politician ...you need not worry over. Your ties with him are cut. Your friend has already entered into another existence; she is no longer of this world. She has gone too, and let it be." Yvette looked over at Celeste's shocked face and said, "In your heart, you knew this, yes Chere?"

Celeste shuddered and told her sister. "You know Yvette, I was really feeling it and had hoped I was wrong, I wanted to be wrong. I wanted Halle to be okay."

Yvette let her know. "Always trust your heart, trust your truth. Don't question knowing, just know." Yvette did not enjoy telling Celeste the rest but continued, "The woman who your ex-husband has made his wife... you need to do a protection spell over. Her mojo is weak and so is her very nature, but her desire is strong so you would do well to protect yourself."

"Are you referring to her desire for Marvin? She has him as her husband now," Celeste responded.

"Yet what she had sought she does not have. She wanted all and everything and knows this is not hers. She blames you for the love he does not have for her, and although she has more than she ever did before, she knows she does not have what you did. It would be best for you to clear her from your mind, for your very thoughts can give her power," Yvette warned.

"I have wanted to do a hex removal or something, but I was unable to do so with clear intentions. I know anything I send out to the universe will come back to me ten-fold, and I don't think I can do anything that concerns her without bad wishes." Celeste hated to even admit that out loud and wished she was a bigger person than that.

"That's honest. We can work with truth. I am going to get some things ready for you, give you some herbs to drink, some items to burn to help yourself be done with this union and the pain and also some protection that I hope will help you to heal," Yvette told her.

Once they returned to Yvette's they began the process. They lit a candle, trying to get into the mindset to do what Celeste believed would be only helpful and good. She drank the tea which was unflavored and so strong, and ate a perfect praline to chase the taste away and then another.

Celeste knew her sister had told her to let it be as far as her friend Halle went, but she had to say something in regards.

"Yvette, on letting Halle's death be... I want to know how? I want to know that those that love her know and that she may be put to rest proper. Also if there are those that did her harm, I want to see them held responsible."

Yvette took a deep breath and said very firmly. "She is gone, it is over. Her choices in her life brought about her death. You must accept this and let it be. There is a God to take care of all of us. What you propose is the Devils work, do not look for revenge, do not try to hold others responsible for wrongs they have done. Know that Karma will do this already. Make right in your own life, spread love and good in all you do. That is what is best, live your life well sister."

   Celeste knew anymore conversation on this would only frustrate Yvette, and she did not need to have repeated what she had already heard. Hearing something and knowing it is right is one thing. Doing it? Well, doing it would be harder...

# Chapter 5

The next day Celeste searched her computer for more information, particularly regarding Halle. She believed her sister. When Yvette had spoken the words, she felt them to be true. Yet she wanted to see how, and found nothing. She also tried to call Halle's cell and it was disconnected. That had happened before too from neglecting to pay the bill, but after what Yvette told her she knew the service would not be turned back on.

When Laurent Almonester called, his very voice had Celeste in the mood. She was up for whatever he had in mind. That consisted of a drive, a picnic lunch, and a tour of New Orleans and surrounding areas. Celeste just sat back and listened to him as he pointed out things. He showed her sights and spoke with such passion, such love for the city. Celeste enjoyed his warm voice and felt she could listen to him talk all day long.

Laurent was seventh generation Louisianan and his wife had been a Georgian girl who died far too young from cancer. They had not had any children. He possessed a quiet sadness, a palpable sense of loss, but yet such an acceptance on life as it were. Celeste felt feelings for him that were crazy strong considering they had only met the evening before. She felt at total ease in his company. They did not need pretense or airs, no need to size each other up or play any kind of games. They enjoyed being together and wanted to be together.

Laurent had been in mourning for the loss of his wife, and certainly there was no shortage of female interest. He had not lived as a hermit; he loved women and their company. With Celeste something clicked into place, rather chemistry, God's divine plan, he did not know. To only have such a short time together was not going to be enough for him though, of that he was certain.

For Celeste she was drawn to Laurent with feelings too strong to deny, rather or not it lasted past this visit she did not know but when he took her to his home and laid her on his bed she wanted him right then, and that's what they had.

Laurent continued to kiss Celeste. He moved from her mouth to her neck, caressing her breast at the same time. When his mouth found her nipple she felt a surge travel through her body and moaned with pleasure. She wanted all of her clothes off and his too. Needing to feel his skin next to hers, she pulled at his shirt. Then after opening it, he lifted her dress over her head and then undid her bra. She clung to him and kissed him deeply wrapping her legs around his body to hold him close.

His mouth and hands traveled down her body, cupping her ass and then lifting her up to pull off her panties, taking his pants off then too. Laurent left no part of Celeste untouched, and she responded to him hungrily. They kissed deeply, ran their hands over the other's body in a sensual dance in tune with each other. When his fingers felt her wetness, gently rubbing on her she almost came just that fast.

Her body was built up with tension and desire. She tried to pull him to her, but he held her hands and slid down between her legs, using his tongue to take her over the edge. Celeste called out his name. His hands held her pelvis in place while he lifted her, her legs were spread, and his lips were sucking the sweet juices as her body was having spasms that he was in full control of.

There was something so sexy about a man in control. One who could handle a woman and bring her pleasure. Celeste could tell it was exactly what he wanted; she felt no inhibitions, no shyness, or shame.

He began stroking her, tenderly licking her clitoris and kissing her inner thighs, fingering her breasts. He was touching her in places she did not even know she needed him to, in places that she hungered for the sensual touch of a man.

As another wave of pleasure began, he slipped a condom on and entered her slowly, smoothly. The walls of her vagina were silky wet and ready for him. Her orgasm intensified. He moved slowly, stroking her, not pulling all the way out. She loved that. Just a good easy fuck, which had her coming again...

"Laurent, oh fuck," she moaned as she clung to him as her muscles contracted on his cock inside of her. It felt so good. Her orgasm seemed to ebb, to ease up, and only to build once more as his strokes increased. His cock became swollen and throbbed inside of her as he also came hard.

One might think that this would leave them both sated and done for the evening, having found such beautiful release and satisfaction. Instead, it seemed that something had awakened in them both and they craved more of each other.

As they continue to kiss, embrace, and touch, Celeste ended up on top of Laurent. Her body was lying on him. Her tongue was circling his nipples and then onto his belly, and finally to his beautiful male organ. She used the tip of her tongue to circle the tip of his cock, and then her lips circling just the tip in a kiss and then a suck and a pull as she took more of the cock into her mouth and then backed up. Only her tongue was running down the backside of his thick beautiful dark cock. He enjoyed it, but wanted to be inside of her again so she put on another condom and rode him, as he rubbed her clit and made her come again. Then they reversed positions. Laurent lifted her legs and fucked her so good and so steady a pressure built up inside of her that almost felt like she had to pee, but she didn't hold back. She squirted in a female ejaculation that was so much more than just an orgasm. It was that too, but times ten. The feelings and release took her to a whole other place. For some amount of time she simply lost her mind in the most glorious fashion.

Somewhere in the background she heard John Hiatts' sexy voice singing, *"It Feels like Rain."* She knew Laurent, her, and the bed were soaked.

He pulled her with him to the other side of his big bed and she faded into blissful sleep, waking in the morning in the very same position.

Such a total surprise, with her husband they had lain together, but always separated to sleep. Here, she was in total comfort on his chest. His arm was around her and he nuzzled her hair with a kiss. Somehow, they found themselves making love gently that morning. Just as easy and natural as could be.

It was so unbelievably natural and comfortable with this man. It was amazing to Celeste how right it felt. For how Celeste was feeling it was like they had known each other so much longer.

They showered, had coffee and sat outside breathing in all that was good. It was pleasant here. She could see why he called this home, and she felt so at ease.

Laurent presented her with a few CD's for her long drive home. He included a piece of paper with his address and phone number, and Celeste made certain to write hers out for Laurent as well.

This would be her last day there, and she would take off early the next day. Yvette actually wanted her to leave by the light of the full moon, rather than after the sun rose.

Celeste held Laurent's hand and they sat there grinning at each other until they both laughed. There was a connection, and they really did not need to fill it in with a bunch of words or proclamations. They would know each other, they would share...she already knew she would carry a piece of him in her heart.

It struck Celeste a little funny, that so often people got out of a relationship and while still in pain did a replacement to stop hurting, just to fill the void. She had not thought that was the healthiest way and had not wanted that for herself. Hell, she could not have even imagined it. Then all out of the blue, not even looking, clear across the country she stepped into a yard, spotted Laurent and was drawn like a fish to water.

He drove her back to the Quarter.

"Au Revoir"...until we meet again," he uttered kissing her lips...

# Chapter 6

Yvette and Celeste had a quiet evening. Celeste shared about her time with Laurent some and Yvette told her about a lover she had taken recently. They called it an early night, since 5am would come early.

Celeste had her car loaded, with a little black angel figurine to ride with her from Yvette, and also a soft little bag against her breasts with herbs inside and a crystal.

"Life itself is magic. All of creation is a miracle, and every person on Earth is a spiritual being having a human experience," Those were Yvette's parting words.

With a hug full of love and a heart full of gratitude Celeste began her journey home.

She drove about an hour and a half west on the I-10, then another hour on the I-190 and stopped to refresh before she did another three hours north on the I-49 and crossed into Texas. Having biscuits and gravy at another stop, she continued a few hours more into Oklahoma.

It was 5:00 in the evening. It had been a twelve hour day when she stopped for the night off the Indian Nation Turnpike. She had hoped to stay at the casino, but instead ended in a low budget motel with a McDonald's dinner. She put a chair at an angle against the door and pinned the drapes to block out light.

Internet was terrible, so Celeste gave that up. She read a Jackie Collins novel for hours until sleep came.

The next morning, she was relieved to be leaving that hell hole. She was anxious to get back on her drive. The neighbors looked sketchy, hell, everywhere she looked felt sketchy and she felt stared at. It gave her the creeps; she had done some hotel room coffee, hit the road for three hours crossing into Kansas, and then stopped for fuel and a decent meal.

Electing to have a good solid meal, she was able to get on the internet to check her route. She had hoped to cross into Colorado before the day was done, but instead decided on Hays, Kansas.

Gassed up and well fed, Celeste sung out loud with Buddy Guy and then Etta James. She had played Dwight Yoakum through Oklahoma. She loved good country, as well as good soulful blues.

The sights changed throughout her drive, her mind wandered back over the events in Washington D.C. It really felt further behind her than seemed possible. Maybe that was because foremost on her mind, what consumed the hours on the road was Laurent. Replaying those memories, it was all she could do not to touch herself. She was sure a huge smile was evident. That man made her feel good...Period.

Also on her mind was getting home and being able to find a house to buy. All she did on her own. No one could ever take that from her. What a relief, what a total blessing this would be. To never have to worry over rent or worry over not having a place to live, or her grown kids or grandbabies either if they needed. She wanted to be able to leave something for them.

This gave her a feeling of contentment she had never experienced before. She knew each and every day of the rest of her life; gratitude could be found in this.

The drive was boring, so she stopped for the night in Hays Kansas to rest and refresh. Celeste mapped out the remainder of her trip, deciding to drive to Denver the next day which would be about five hours of road time. Her body was feeling the toll of sitting for long hours, having to hold herself in the same position, and she felt a lot better having a definite spot to get to.

It was here that she searched the internet and found that Halle's body had been discovered, behind dumpsters at a work site in Fairfax Virginia a few days earlier. She had been identified and foul play was suspected.

"Foul play." Celeste said the words out loud. What an odd term. She had already been told Halle had passed and already wrapped her mind around it some, but to see it plain and in words in front of her did bring tears. What a waste, what a sad ending. Celeste pondered there were more sad endings than happy ones, and the life Halle had lived often did not conclude with a fairy tale ending. Still, it could have, and Celeste grieved for what she wished had been.

Again in her life, the lesson of wanting for others does not make it be. Each person had to make things happen on their own, take their own roads, their own journey.

Celeste lit a candle and had a good cry for the loss of her friend and possibilities unmet and then found a meeting in the Denver area. She knew it had been too long since being in a meeting and she desired to be around people she had something in common with that she could listen to and talk to. She found herself an A.A. meeting, and was so grateful for the hugs. The unconditional love that was given to her, anytime, and anywhere she walked into the rooms of a twelve step meeting.

She was so very grateful for God's blessings, for the recovery of her disease of addiction. No matter where in the world she was, in the twelve step rooms she was with other recovering people, her people, and all of them miracles…

# Chapter 7

The next morning Celeste hit an eye opening meeting, soaking up the recovery, and even joined some of the crowd for breakfast following the meeting. She chose a German pancake with butter, lemon juice and powdered sugar.

The combination was such a delight, and paired well with the crisp bacon. The people with her were warm and friendly. She enjoyed more the listening to them, than participating in conversations, but of course was asked about her road trip. It was cool, she said what she was comfortable saying, got and gave some much needed hugs. Afterwards Celeste got some Starbucks and hit the road to Salt Lake City. Today would be about eight hours driving, the next day would bring a shorter time behind the wheel.

The drive was fantastic, beautiful sights, clear weather. Celeste felt refreshed and optimistic. There was a voicemail too from Laurent. The man did not own a computer or a cell phone, she had to smile. Some might view that as out of date, but Celeste realized he just did not create a need when it was not there. His life, his world was simpler, more laid back.

She pondered over this again, thinking of her life and her future and Laurent in it. In what form, she didn't know. Her mind wandered over the miles and the hours behind the wheel, to them visiting cross country... to them cohabitating, setting up house, living happily ever after. In these fantasies as she travelled, she also re-played their lovemaking session and thought about waking next to him again and again. Yep, she was sure enough feeling Laurent.

That evening, as she entered Salt Lake City, she admired the beautiful country side. She understood how travelers could decide this was where they would settle. The place had a real good vibe for her. She walked to a little restaurant and had a paperback with her as well to keep company. Only two more days and she would be home. She had to laugh to herself, no more road trips for this gal. Having done Canada, California and Nevada before, but never alone; this alone cross country stuff was not what was up.

A woman could enjoy her alone time and her own company. Fine, she was with that, but too doggone many hours continuously, she was so not feeling all that.

The next day was shorter; about five hours drive time to Boise Idaho, which was her last stop before heading home to Portland. Boise was way cooler than she would have thought. The downtown area was pretty and felt lively. She found a massage school to get a nice massage at and her body loved her for it. Enjoying what at this point felt like a shorter day.

She browsed a book store finding some goodies as well, John Grisham and Phillip Margolin would go home with her. Phillip was a Portlander. He had been a practicing attorney that wrote novels based in the Portland area, so Celeste loved reading everything he wrote. As far as John Grisham, well the man could just tell a story. That was all there was to that.

This was the last evening on the road. Oh, how she looked forward to getting to her own bed the next day.

Before she showered and cracked open a new book, she searched properties in the Portland area. Having called St Johns, which was located in North Portland, home for so many years but knew prices were up on what were really smaller homes for the most part. Still she continued to look, hopeful, and then she expanded her look. Vancouver was so not an option but it was hard to do searches that eliminated the area, even though it was in the State of Washington, it came up over and over again.

She ruled out the Beaverton area and on the other side of town, Gresham was a little further than she wanted. She looked at lower NE, higher numbers, Park Rose and Happy Valley. She contacted a realtor and they sat up a get together for that coming Friday. She hoped things would end in her finding the home of her dreams.

Calling to let her kids know she would be home by the following evening. She told them too that their Aunt Yvette was buying a home in Oregon and that Celeste was going to find it for her. She figured her kids did not need to hear all the details that had led to this, and it was accepted with excitement from all of them.

They were still reeling from the brand new car mama would be driving home. Celeste would refer to a benefactor in D.C. She would say he had supplied this and would supply living costs to cover her for the next year, at the least, If not two. After her house purchase and $100,000.00 in investments, she figured $50,000 should last pretty good. Of course, there would be purchases for the new home but she promised herself to go easy and take it slow. Too many folks got some money and went through it in lightning speed and she was determined not to be one of them...

# Chapter 8

The next day Celeste was so anxious to get home. She was focused. She watched the miles and watched the clock, and was so glad to park the ride outside her apartment complex at 4:00 pm. She dragged all the bags into the apartment in three trips and opened windows and the sliding back patio door, the place needed some serious airing out.

Savannah jumped up on her lap purring as soon as Celeste sat down. Her cat let her know she was glad to have her home. Shannel had come over to let her in or out while Celeste was gone away. She made sure food and water was inside, as well as on the patio in the back, even though there were strays in the area.

Matter of fact, it could be called a stray problem. One female that was not spayed could have a couple litters of kittens each year, and those kittens could be getting pregnant three to six months later. It did not take long for a major problem to evolve, even with a high mortality rate.

She was never ever going to miss this apartment, not a single day. Since buying a house took six weeks if all ran smooth, she so wanted to find her new place fast. She decided to give the manager here at the apartments a two month notice and extend if she must.

Celeste was so excited to be home and have a new adventure to dive into. She unpacked, started a load of laundry, and invited Shannel and her baby girl over. Then Celeste ordered pizza and started in emptying the fridge, filling a trash bag.

It was fantastic to see her youngest girl and her little baby. She enjoyed catching up on the goings on in both of their lives. The girls stayed a while and she sent them home with some pizza and a bag of souvenirs, and hit her computer again. She searched and chose a few houses she wanted to take a look at, and sent her realtor an email.

It was such a fantastic blessing to sleep in her own bed. She lay down on her firm pillow top mattress, pulling high thread count sheets and down comforter over herself and snuggling in for a restful night's sleep. She ached some in the morning, but figured that was to be expected after the week she had just had with so many hours sitting tense in her car.

Celeste had a stack of mail to go through and she saw a letter from Marvin, as well as a letter from Laurent. She chose to open Laurent's first and marveled at how things had changed for her, an attitude adjustment really.

Marvin no longer had to be the last thing she thought of at night, or what kept her awake all night. No more disturbed dreams, just peaceful rest. He did not need to be the first thing she thought of when she woke either, and maybe someday she would even have a full entire day without him coming to her mind. That would be nice, because thoughts of him still hurt her.

She opened Laurent's letter. *'Oh goodness. A man that actually took the time to write a letter, and he expressed himself well.'* He let her know the impact she had made in his life and that he would love to come visit her. Saying that whenever she was ready, to let him know. She had a smile on her face and felt so happy.

To be wanted was a pretty basic need really. Of course a woman did not have to have a man to be complete or to have a full life, but then again having one sure made it more fun.

'And Marvin, really?' He had the audacity to send some financial information on an old debt he paid off. Woopty damn doo. A little note hoping she was doing well. That was it! After all those years together, all those shared times and memories, he hoped she was doing well! She shook her head and tore up the entire envelope. No return address, typical passive aggressive bullshit, and here she had let him get all the way under her skin.

Celeste was sobbing as she tore the paper and really wished she had an off button to press. A *'no feelings,' 'stop feelings'* button. Damn it, not even back twenty four hours and she was in an emotional place she did not want to be. What the hell was wrong with her? At that moment she hated him.

A thin line between love and hate, it was a well-known verse. Sung about, put into poems and even talked about. It was so very true. The harder, deeper, more intense and passionate the love was felt... then the more deeply the venomous, vile and deep hate was on the other side. She felt like shit.

Celeste splashed cold water on her face. She dried her face and put on lotion. She got dressed and went into St Johns, getting an iced mocha on her drive out to Valerie and Kenny Rays. She wanted to see them and the kids, and give those gifts from her travels. Tourist gifts such as Snow globes, magnets, shot glasses, bells and T-shirts. They talked about some house plans. They very much wanted her to move out towards them, and Valerie had been looking for her as well, and had some listings for her to check out.

It was so fantastic to see her daughter happy and their household together. Her daughter was so upbeat, and as always, Kenny Ray had plans and ideas. She laughed and listened easily and really enjoyed her family. She felt so very lucky and grateful.

Celeste had written down a few addresses and she drove by to check them out and get a feel for the neighborhoods. She ruled two out, not even wanting to go inside. One had been so gorgeous from the pictures, cherry red built-in's, formal dining room, style and personality. When she drove by she found that it was kitty corner to a strip club and had low rent apartments lining the street. She was so disappointed; it had been her favorite from the internet photos.

Over the course of the day she had tried to hook up with her son Michael, but his schedule prevented it, so she invited him and his little family over for Sunday dinner.

When Celeste went to the store to get food back in her apartment, she picked up an Oregon postcard to send to Laurent right away. She also got some boxes, packing tape and newspaper. Figuring she would start in on boxing stuff up. On her way home, she dropped another grand in the bank to transfer to her investment account.

She was feeling thrilled, renewed even, thinking of Laurent. This cross country potential romance had some pluses. She could see why women liked to have male pen pals behind bars. They had time to write sweet letters, they looked forward to hearing from a woman, and you knew where the men were.

Okay, well Laurent was a free man. That was just one of the differences. Even still, that is what crossed her mind. It was fun, the lost art of snail mail. The waiting to communicate, the thought put into it, the anticipation of going to the mailbox and opening something from someone who had taken the time to write words with his own hands.

The thoughts from his own mind, he wrote a woman's name and gave thought to her as he mailed it. This was almost a lost art. She wasn't sure if her granddaughters would even know this. Would they get to experience this? She was glad for her age and maturity. She had been young, been there, done that, and where she was at right now, at this point in her life was pretty damn good.

It was cool to be back in her apartment. She clicked on the TV to keep her company while writing out a postcard for Laurent. She then browsed the web and checked on the five houses she planned to get inside to view the next morning...

# Chapter 9

By Sunday, fourteen houses had been viewed. There were three being seriously considered, but none were without drawbacks. There was horrendous wallpaper or outdated bathrooms or questionable layouts. It was just that none felt really right.

Still, she looked over pictures and her notes, and thought about them. She pictured herself living there and considered. She figured Valerie would go with her the following week to look at these three again and she also had some more scheduled.

*****

Michael, Annabella and their son came for dinner. Celeste had made spring rolls, stir fry, short ribs and rice. It was a relaxing evening. Annabella was a doting mother. Being a wife and mommy seemed to suit her. She had a confidence Celeste had never seen in her before and their son seemed happy. They opened their souvenirs and marveled at the number of states Celeste had driven through and admired the new ride.

It got a little uncomfortable when the subject of a cousins wedding came up. Michael seemed to be choosing his words carefully.

"Mom, you know Dad said he and Carmine were going and I just don't want you to be blindsided."

"Oh honey, I'm glad you let me know. It will be a little uncomfortable, sure, but I am not going to let that stop me from seeing my niece get married. Matter of fact, I'm thinking perhaps I should bring an escort with me as well," Celeste told him, the idea just now forming in her mind. But as she spoke the words, deciding maybe it was a good idea after all.

"Oh yeah? ...Who you got in mind Mama?" Michael asked with a pleasant smile.

"Well, when I was in New Orleans, I spent some time with a man that would like to come out and visit. If all goes right with getting into a house, the timing might be perfect for him to come out after I move in and go to the wedding with me. But you know it's just a thought. We'll see."

"Okay then Mama, you go ahead," Michael laughed, but seemed to be pleased to hear his Mother talking about having company.

After her son and his family left, she sat down to write Laurent a letter. She wanted to tell him about her house hunting, how she missed him and how she would love him to come out and stay a while after the move. She also mentioned the upcoming wedding, even though she still had some mixed feelings. One of the things she really did not want to happen is Laurent to go anywhere with her, and Marvin be there and try to befriend him. She could picture Marvin shaking his hands and a male buddy thing occurring. There was nothing about that scenario that she was feeling for sure.

Life had somehow gotten more complicated. There were new roles with someone who had shared her life with her. Her partner was now someone else's husband.

She so did not want to see this female, and did not really want Laurent to be around either one of them. In a situation like that, her private thoughts would love to show up and show out.

Damn it, when she was out of town with so much more going on, all this seemed more distant. With a client falling over dead and a million bucks in his closet...there were other things to focus on. With Halle winding up dead and then finding a new lover, a man she felt she was falling in love with, all this kept her brain in over drive. Now, being back home with a house to buy and boxes to pack up, what the hell were Marvin and Carmine taking up mental space for? She felt disgust with herself. So many people seemed to do all this so much easier than she seemed to be able to.

She realized with frustration that she still loved Marvin. Probably always would and didn't think she would ever be able to see him with Carmine and feel okay.

Celeste went and got her protection bag that she had worn on the drive across country. The small bag had been worn close to her heart, inside of it was a blend herbs had been placed. Often protection bags included bone, crystals, whatever was thought to be helpful to the wearer for their own purposes.

Yvette had helped to prepare a travel bag for her sister. Celeste knew it needed to be buried once its use was completed. She sent an email to Yvette letting her know where she was at emotionally, and asking what might be good to include in taking care of herself. Especially since it seemed that she would find herself at the same location as Carmine in the near future.

Yvette replied that she should nurture herself and not give Carmine or Marvin extra thoughts. She said that the best thing to do would be, "To pray for them each and every night for two weeks straight, even if you don't mean it sincerely."

Celeste knew she made a face in spite of herself. *'Be careful what you ask for,'* she thought. This was not something she wanted to do, nor did she want to get willing to do it. Not at this point anyway.

She set about smudging her apartment room by room with sage that was burning in her abalone shell. It was done to remove negative feelings and influences. She then got out a long braid of sweet grass and went through the rooms again to bring about positive energy after the cleansing. After that, she lit frankincense and myrrh that were kept on hand and dug a hole outside bury her protection bag that had been worn during her drive home. The symbolic rituals of healing and practicing spirituality helped. She lit a candle and sat quietly, breathing in good thoughts and ideals and breathing out that which troubled her, giving it to God and asking for the help needed…

# Chapter 10

There were many houses viewed in the days that followed, reviewing her notes about them after was a tiring process. There were homes that were vacant with trash left behind and houses with people still living there and present while she looked, which was an odd experience. Each and every house had something that she hated on sight or something that just did not feel right.

Soon enough, she located the house that would be perfect. It was in a north east neighborhood, and when she walked in it was love. Everything about the house was great. There was crown molding, fabulous built-ins, and a big stone fireplace. As she went down the hall to the master bedroom Celeste saw that there were French doors off of her bedroom, which included a seating area.

She was in love. The place was move-in ready, and it was the best home she had walked into.

There were so many phone calls and papers needing signed, faxes, and inspections. It was an exhausting process, but Celeste had been through it before so she knew the fun part was looking casually. All the rest of it was stressful and busy, but at least now she knew she was in the end zone and would be a home owner soon.

Celeste rung Laurent up and he answered with a simple, "Hello?" That made her smile. His voice was so smooth and sexy to her that a simple hello was enough to have her squeezing her legs together. "Hi Laurent, it's so good to hear your voice."

"Oh bebe, you too. You sound happy. I can hear you smiling through your voice," he chuckled.

"That's because I'm talking to you, so how flexible is your schedule? I want some company in my big ole house once I get moved in." When she laughed, it sounded like chimes to Laurent.

"I am very ready, just waiting on you to tell me when. That's a huge benefit from being my own boss," he spoke without hesitation.

They set a time frame and Celeste let him know she would look on the internet at flights. She would pick a good one for him and get back to him.

Laurent had a pilot's license, these days doing local scenic flights around the bayou. He also played music with various musicians at gigs for fun mostly and he carved wood. She had seen some of the pieces and could say first hand she knew how good his hands were. Good hands and a good sexy voice.

She looked forward to hearing him sing. Celeste honestly had not found a single thing to not dig about this man. It amazed her how much of a match they seemed to be and how easy just talking with him felt. Even these short conversations filled her world, completed parts of her, and gave her something she didn't even know she wanted.

*****

Once a closing date was set, she got real serious about boxing up all her belongings except what was absolutely needed to be used before moving. She rented a truck. Moving day help was arranged, and one week later she would be going to the airport and picking up Laurent to bring him to her new home.

Thankfully, her son had a few friends to come help move. With Kenny Ray's help and a hand truck, her storage unit was emptied and her new garage filled up. She put her bed in the new guest room.

She had big plans for what would grace her enormous master bedroom. The room came complete with a sitting area, walk in closet, large nicely done bathroom and even a small fireplace. Celeste wanted to put a large four poster king size bed in this room. It could handle it and so could she.

Knowing it would take days to get the essentials unpacked and put away, she certainly had time and wasn't on anybody else's schedule. As clothes were hung in the closet, she marveled at the space and no sharing either. This house was crazy big for one person, but had a good flow to it and felt homey and comfortable.

Celeste knew with grandkid sleepovers and the more her family grew, they could always make enough room here for everybody too. She liked having options and loved that she did not need to run nothing by nobody. She did not need permission or even anyone else's opinion.

The freedom felt was incredible. Never in her life had she felt anything close to what she was experiencing now. Her options felt limited only by her own imagination. She owned a home! Free and clear. She would never ever have to worry about where to live, making rent, or divorce. She would never again suffer through someone's using drugs in her space, making her dwelling feel unsafe or compromised.

Celeste believed at that moment that she would never in her life give away her power or freedom. She would never let a man cause her unhappy days and worried nights, even if that meant being single the rest of her life, then so be it because the tradeoff was not worth it. It had all come down too damn hard before.

That first night once everyone left, there were some creepy moments. House settling creaks and the freezer was making its noises. Branches brushed against the house. It was a new neighborhood for her and with it came new sounds.

Her senses seemed to be on high alert. She really wanted to relax, and was thankful that at least her body was tired. She hoped that her mind would unwind and relax as well. When she lay down that night in the guest bedroom, it really was a similar size of the apartment she had slept in the night before. As Celeste said her prayers, they were extra full of gratitude. A dream had come true. A blessing, that was so very large in her mind. After she and Marvin had lost their home together, it had seemed like owning another would not be in the cards for her, and here she was. Hallelujah!

# Chapter 11

She did a deep red paint job in the master. A king size, four poster Tempurpedic bed had also been set up in the bedroom. It was all coming together. Home...Not just a house, but home, and so very much more.

By the time she arrived at the airport, Celeste was overjoyed. Her kids had asked way more questions about Laurent than she ever had on their romantic choices. Celeste did not want them to come over and take stock and scrutinize too quickly. It had been a little work, but she had persuaded them to wait until the housewarming party to come and meet Laurent. A group of people would be over, which Celeste felt would take the pressure off Laurent and the setting would be a more casual, social event.

Celeste and Laurent had six nights to spend together alone before the house warming with no interference, nothing but just the two of them, and that was exactly what Celeste wanted. Pulling up in front of baggage claim and there he was. Celeste stopped her car, jumped out and threw herself into his arms. He was ready and waiting. Their embrace was heartfelt and she laughed. How did this man have her laughing, grinning and gushing every time she heard his voice or saw him?

Some kind of wonderful had overtaken her and she decided to just go with it. Celeste kissed Laurent, and let him go, opening her trunk for his luggage. God, he looked good, here in Portland, here with her.

When they got back to her new home, Celeste gave him a tour. He was impressed and they talked about ideas and things she would like to do.

"I'm totally down on helping you. I've never been to a home depot and I'd look forward to the outing," he admitted.

"You are my kind of man Laurent. For real? We'll see, I mean it would be fun for me, but you got to have a good time while you're here."

"Spending time with you is a good time, and helping you do things around here would give me great pleasure. Girl, I wouldn't say it if I didn't mean it."

While standing in one of the four bedrooms, Laurent asked if she had plans for it. She did let him know, "I would love a library. One of the houses I had looked at had one, built in shelves lining the walls. I think this room would be perfect as a library."

"Let's do it, let's build you a library. You know I can work some wood, I can make you some special to order beautiful shelves, alright?" Laurent seemed so sincere and pleased with himself, Celeste was thrilled.

"Yes. Oh Laurent yes, that sounds truly wonderful. I would love it. Let's, let's make it happen."

"For now, let's make some dinner happen. I got some nice steaks in the fridge, thinking a big salad to go with, does that sound alright?" Celeste asked as they walked to the kitchen.

"That sounds more than alright. You got a grill out there? How about you let me fire it up and get those steaks right and you do the salad?" he suggested.

What was it about all men wanting to cook outdoors? Was it something primal? She pointed out what he would need, and started in on slicing strawberries for the 7 UP pound cake and whipped cream dessert. She made a big salad leaving off the dressing, to be added later.

Man, those steaks were smelling great and cooked to perfection. The meal was simple and perfect. They ate outside, enjoying the lack of humidity that Oregon offered compared to Louisiana. They drank iced cold water, and took their fill of the meal. Laurent suggested a neighborhood walk.

"Really?" Celeste considered. "I have not done that, but sure we can. No doubt it would do me good."

So, they did wind up taking a stroll. It was pleasant to be in no hurry and just walk under the trees, and down side streets in what was now Celeste's neighborhood. Having never had a dog, she was not used to just walking the neighborhood. Oh, she saw dog walkers, power walkers and others do it but somehow it had never been something she did, such a simple thing really.

"Don't the English call this their constitutional?" Celeste laughed.

"I have heard that before, I just call it walking. How can you say you live in this great place and not take yourself some beautiful walks?" Laurent asked.

"I don't know, we get so much rain, and when I need to go somewhere I drive, like drive to the park then walk, whatever. Don't even think I am going to turn into a hiker, okay? I'll just go ahead and put that out there now."

Laurent laughed. "I can understand that, a step at a time, alright? Don't even think I am trying to change anything about you. I just thought a walk through your neighborhood would be good, check it out. Let everyone see you got a big strong man with you too."

"Oh hush, Laurent," Celeste said laughing too, he might have been half playing and the other half serious, but it was said casual enough and besides, she liked it.

When they returned from their walk Laurent suggested she find some internet pictures of custom made book shelves she liked. Celeste of course chose antique styles. She preferred an old money style. She liked the vintage way of starting at the ceiling, and going all the way down to the floor, with a cherry color to them. Not a light oak or a dark wood. Laurent said he thought he had a pretty good feel of what she wanted. They had strawberry shortcake and he took a tablet, measuring tape and pencil to the bedroom where the library would be and made some measurements and wrote notes to himself.

That night when they went to bed, it was natural they made love with a sweet passion. Their kisses were hungry and desire built within them both. When this man entered her she felt such pleasure. "ummmm" Celeste moaned. Yes! More and deep as he wanted, her body was ready for everything he had.

They slept with a ceiling fan going, creating a soft breeze over their bodies. Throughout the night one or the other would adjust themselves, and reach out to kiss or touch the other in acknowledgement.

The next morning, Celeste woke to the smell of coffee and bacon. Laurent was in the middle of making flapjacks and had the table set. Celeste pulled her arms around him and leaned in from behind him kissing his shoulder. She then poured a mug of black coffee and headed to the deck to enjoy her morning ritual of coffee and a good cigarette.

Normally needing at least an hour or two in the morning before she faced food, but then again when a man was up and cooking in the morning she figured she better get with that. And the aromas did have a way of bringing on an appetite.

After breakfast, they went and rented a truck from U-Haul, then continued on the adventure of supply shopping. Entering the enormous Home Depot store that was popular in the Northwest part of the country, Laurent was in awe.

Cherry wood was not cheap, but boy was it beautiful. Laurent had looked at her small supply of tools prior to their shopping trip so had a list of what was needed; she would be the owner of a saw before the day was out.

Laurent wanted to make sure that it was a one trip mission, and Celeste left him to it while she wandered the plant and garden section. She chose a hedger, two peach trees, a cherry blossom tree, lilac bush, and a water fountain and some decorative stones. She had plans in mind, and figured while there was a truck and someone to help unload she was going for it.

At check-out Laurent was trying to pay for the entire load. Celeste suggested, "Laurent, man you are doing all the work. I should get the supplies."

He leaned toward her, and said in her ear, "I want to do this, and the way to really give you a total gift is to let me totally do it." Celeste said "At least let's split it?" He shook his head no, used a card, and tried to get the cashier to ring the garden stuff onto his bill too.

"No, no I got the garden stuff," Celeste spoke firmly.

Was this their first fight? Wow, what a great first fight she thought, fussing about him wanting to pay for the whole load. Well one thing she knew for certain, he had some money and some credit, like a grown man should.

Once they were back home and everything was unloaded, Celeste said she would return the truck and get some chicken, giving him the chance to get started.

He came up and got a plate once she returned, and then they both got busy. She headed to the backyard and he made his way to what was to become the library. Soulful rhythm and blues filled the space, and she was comfortably in her zone when she sensed him nearby. He handed her an iced peach tea and commented, "It is so nice out here. I think I could use an outdoor break, how about I set the fountain up for you?"

"Not much of a break but you talked me into it! Where were you thinking?" He pointed to the same spot she had in mind and he set about opening and installing, and thankfully let her be, with her chores as well. Celeste had to marvel at being with a man who did not have the need to oversee and obviously think a man could do better. He never once looked at her or what she was doing as if it or she could be better.

She had a flashback of all her years with Marvin. It was true that he always accepted her, no matter her size or her dreams or desires. But, it was also true that he worried her to death about needing to talk details and explain over again and question if she knew for sure how she was doing something. The truth was a whole lot of what needed done just required reading and following directions. Hell, she could do that.

Once the plants had a certain depth of a hole, and distance between them, she added a good soil mix and it was pretty straightforward. Celeste had enjoyed having a garden before, and she desired either food producing or flowering to grace her yard. She knew the next year she would be starting much earlier in the season.

Finally exhausted with sun, soil and sweat, she took a cooling shower and did a shampoo too before putting on a summer dress with nothing underneath it. She ventured back to the room that was to be a library to check out Laurent's wood work. "Wow! I can't believe how much you got done. It looks amazing." She stroked the wood, two solid shelf frames side by side, firmly in place. It was already looking gorgeous. "Laurent these are fantastic."

"You sound surprised, these are just the bones, I'll get the shelves installed tomorrow and some detail finishing's and then two coats to follow with dry time, but yeah I'm pleased." Laurent said, wiping his hands on a rag. "Now I think I'm due for a shower myself."

Celeste hooked up a pasta salad with chicken and shrimp while Laurent was in the shower. They enjoyed it in front of the TV, watching "The Sopranos." When it finished, she realized Laurent was asleep and smiled to herself. All men could do that, just fall asleep anywhere. She let him sleep, covering him with a blanket and locked up the house.

Celeste went into the kitchen to set the coffee pot for the morning, before going into her bedroom to read, she knew he would join her, so she let him sleep.

Sometime during the night she was aware of his coming to bed, although she had not recalled waking completely. In the morning when she woke, she thought again at how comfortable they both seemed to be with each other.

It was a beautiful thing to not have to worry over if he felt okay or if she was safe enough to sleep. Because she had lived during times like that, her mind flashed on how very different she felt today.

In her many years with Marvin, she had always had trouble falling asleep when he wasn't home. If she woke and he was gone, like on so many occasions she had felt a fear and a need to seek him out. That was no longer her life. Any part of that was only past memories. Celeste knew people took old baggage into new relationships, it would be expected. What a feeling of relief to realize that with this man asleep in her bed she did not have any of those thoughts, or flashes of bad feelings that had been such a part of her life. It was the very absence of that that had her recalling what her past had been.

Maybe a big part is that when women picked their men, they went for what they knew. Celeste felt like God put her and Laurent in each other's path. It happened at the right time and in the right way. Laurent was definitely on her gratitude list, and every night when she said her prayers it was gratitude she started with. So many small things made such a big impact in her life…

# Chapter 12

"Good morning beautiful." Laurent came out to the deck, a cup of coffee in his hand. "Cool to join you? Or are you trying to have time to yourself?"

"I love your company, Have a seat. You know I was just thinking how nice it is to share this time together and feel soooo at ease. I felt so comfortable last night, I just left you asleep on the couch," she chuckled.

"It's all good. I'm glad you did, don't worry about me baby, I been grown a long time." He looked at her and continued, "It's actually really nice to be with a woman secure enough in herself to not have to worry over me. I don't want you feeling any kind of way, like you have to entertain me or not do what you normally do because I'm here, this is your world, do you."

"Man, glad to hear it. You know I been feeling so good about everything, digging our vibe together. So nice to hear you say out loud what I am feeling," Celeste let him know. She went back in to refill her coffee. Joining him again, she said, "You know I do go to twelve step meetings on the regular, thinking of going to one tonight, you interested?"

"Well I never have been a drinker. I've seen a lot of others do it and what I saw didn't work out that well for them, so me, I just chose not to. I like to do what they say... keep it real. Real feelings, not alcohol fortified. Folks get more lose with drinks, but meaner too, and sloppier. It just was nothing I ever wanted." He leaned over to Celeste and gave her a kiss and continued. "I like that you don't drink; now because you did, hell I don't fault you. I try not to sit in judgment on others, point in fact I feel real pride that you found your way out of it and live without alcohol. So, by all means go to a meeting, but you don't need to take me, if you're cool with it I can hang out here."

"Alright then. Well this addict is going to hit a meeting then." Celeste took hold of Laurent's hand and he gave hers a squeeze and there they were... grinning at each other again.

\*\*\*\*\*

Progress was made during the day. Boxes were unpacked and discarded by Celeste. Yard work done. Shelves put in by Laurent.

That evening, Celeste went to a good meeting. She knew that a good meeting was one she showed up to with her ears open to listen to others, her heart open to receive the message and speaking when she needed to, sharing what she had to offer.

When she got home, she went to Laurent's arms and began kissing him passionately. Celeste just loved his arms around her. She could stay there for eternity. His hands were sliding down her back to her ass, cupping it and squeezing in sync with what his mouth was doing. She was already in his lap with a dress on, and when she spread her legs apart, her dress hiked up. She rubbed on the hardness beneath his pants, feeling him through her panties and knowing there was warm moisture there and need. She wanted to feel this man inside of her.

She then realized the damn condoms were in the other room. Unprotected sex was not on her agenda, so an interruption was a must. She hurried to grab protection and came back to straddle this man again, riding him smoothly. He felt like he was in very deep in this position and her body ground down to feel every bit of him. He stroked her clitoris while she glided, sliding herself up and down on his manhood. He continued rubbing on her clit at the same time. She came all over him and as he held her in place as he followed with his come throbbing out of his manhood adding warmth inside of the condom.

After they cleaned up, he took her in his arms and sang, *"It feels like rain."* She moved with him and knew she would for the rest of her life, remember this moment. The song had always been a favorite, and she had heard it with him in New Orleans sung by John Hiatt while they lay in bed. Then on the drive home listened to Buddy Guy singing it on a CD Laurent had given her and now this man was singing these beautiful words, and he sounded real good. Celeste felt so fantastic in his arms. They had just had good sex, and this song and dance to follow was another dream come true she had not even known she had...

# Chapter 13

Celeste took Laurent to the coast while the first stain on the shelf units dried. It was only a few hours' drive, but when on the Oregon coast, one always wanted to at least have a hoody in the car. This was not the warm Pacific Ocean of California or Mexico.

The water here was cold and the wind blew hard, but there were always quiet spots to find. While they beach walked, they collected some shells and driftwood. They made their way to Rockaway Beach, where they walked down the streets checking out local shops. They watched salt water taffy being made and bought a wide assortment of flavors to take back to Portland.

They drove down the coast a few miles to hit the town of Garibaldi, so Celeste could let

Laurent discover Oregon myrtle wood. It was a very slow growing tree so it had a lot of natural burls that once polished looked spectacular. She knew that with his appreciation of wood he would love this. The variations ensured that each and every piece would be one of a kind and there was a huge range in shades. Laurent was loving this education and he picked a few items, as well as a book. There was a strong interest developing in his mind on working with this wood. Celeste was going to see if she couldn't make that happen for him in the future.

The next day they drove to Mount Hood, stopping at Frog Lake for a picnic. They checked out the chipmunks that were everywhere, as well as frogs. The water here was nice and the view spectacular. It was also a fairly short drive. Celeste was having fun, loving these cooler spots rather than the heat in the city. She really was enjoying being able to show Laurent and share with him some of her beautiful state of Oregon. They splashed in the water and enjoyed the gorgeous sights.

*****

The following day books were put on her new fabulous gorgeous antique looking shelves. They looked as if they were built with the house, in another century. A dark green wall or another deep red and this room would be set off.

The next day would be the housewarming, and Celeste began preparing pies. Laurent wanted to make gumbo, so she directed him to a store where she hoped he would find everything he was looking for.

*****

The next morning she woke happy and did chores around the house to get it company ready. Celeste was really looking forward to the gathering that would take place, and was delighted when her daughters arrived with their men and babies. She introduced Laurent and suggested.

"You want to take them to show the gorgeous shelves that you made?"

"I would love to. Your mama is pleased with my work, so I'll let this be her brag instead of mine," Laurent replied with a smile, so good natured. Celeste could hear the explanations! The shelves were indeed beautiful, and she greeted family when they returned with a big proud smile. Everyone had comments about them. They were all amazed that such works of art were created in such a short time. Celeste beamed at Valerie and Shannel, so pleased to have her girls here and already liking Laurent.

 With the house filling up and cornbread fresh out the oven, Celeste sat a plate of veggies and ranch out. She added a plate of fried chicken wingettes, and as people arrived other goodies joined the table. Maria brought a platter of tamales, Eva brought a gorgeous dried arrangement and candles, Veronica brought in a plate of cookies and a blue berry bush, and they just kept coming.

 The house was filled with her friends and family taking tours. People were adding to the table, giving hugs and making it a real house warming with extra servings of love.

 The gumbo was on point, and she knew folks were checking out Mr. Laurent Amonester. He seemed comfortable, and joked and bantered with folks. There were some soulful blues on and Laurent broke out his harp and showed out, he was blowing at the same time, and making it all come together. Celeste watched with a big smile. Good music, good people, good food, that was enough. Add Laurent to the mix and it was happiness overload for Celeste. This man was a keeper and such a great addition to her life.

Some more folks arrived a few hours into the party. Finally, Michael and his little family showed up. After that Barbie and Jacks with their group came in.

When Barbie's sons came in Celeste was delighted, she could not see these boy's without smiling. Pablo and Rico were just characters, and had always been so, even as young boys. Baby T came right behind them, and laughter and happy banter made the air vibrant. All of these friends and family were so welcome and so important in Celeste's life.

Some cards got brought out on the large dining table, and it was quickly a full on game of spades. In the kitchen at a built in table, a game of bones got started. The dominos making their familiar sounds with much trash talk going on at both tables. Everyone had a blast. The house was on full. There were so many childhood friends of her kids over, adults now and with their own children and mates, it was fantastic to see them all. Celeste had made a point to have the party be an open invite, and had encouraged her kids to invite as well.

It really was a true blessing to see her kids comfortable with Laurent. She could tell they liked him, and at some point noticed Kenny Ray, Tyrone, Michael and Laurent outside together sitting at the fire pit kicking it. It was wonderful to see this and she felt so happy.

She could smell weed being smoked outside too. Celeste did not mind that, rather she enjoyed the smell and that was one drug that never made her feel like she wanted to use. She had done so much spiritual work with sage, and she felt the smell was very similar, so it just fell into another category for her.

This was the first time ever she had given a party and allowed people to bring any kind of alcohol with them. Celeste felt her spiritual house was in order and that she was okay to allow others to *party* in their own particular way. They could just take it with them when they left, but she did question who the designated driver was. Oregon had a zero tolerance, meaning one drink and it was illegal to drive, so asking who was driving was something people living in this state were well used to.

Celeste offered sleepover couches and the guest bedroom if anyone felt the need or had the desire to crash at her place. She had no takers and her cheeks hurt from smiling. Her throat hurt as well from running her mouth and enthusiastic game playing. She began feeling the soreness by the time she and Laurent bid adieu from her porch, his arm around her and she leaned into him.

"Ahhhh... the last guest off into the night," Celeste said with a tired smile.

"What a fantastic house full of people you had here tonight my dear. This was an enjoyable evening," Laurent replied.

"It was, it really was. It feels kind of perfect," Celeste spoke, with a laugh as they entered back into the house. Food had long been eaten or put away and certainly there was cleaning to do, but instead Celeste suggested they retire and get to it the next morning.

"I like that plan," Laurent agreed. "Let me just check the doors downstairs and make sure everything is secure and I will join you shortly."

Celeste went into her large bathroom, washed her face and applied night cream then brushed her teeth. She removed her clothes and got into bed naked, turning on the ceiling fan and opening two windows for another breeze that would be welcome as the summer evening cooled off.

Laurent came in after having done what he needed to do to prepare for bed and undressed at the bedside. He joined her, naked himself between the soft sheets. She welcomed his body to hers and they began the sensual dance of lovemaking. She cried out his name and clung to him as euphoric bliss overtook her, her body spasms bringing Laurent to his release as well. My God she loved to love this man. Celeste held him, and knew she was right where she wanted to be...

# Chapter 14

The rest of Laurent's visit in Oregon went so quickly. They got together with each one of Celeste's kids and their families separately. It was nice to have more one on one type time for visits and getting acquainted. Kenny Ray and Michael both really liked Laurent, and he liked them as well. Celeste was grateful for that. Her daughters had good things to say about Laurent too, she knew they had been leery and protective of their Mother and concerned on who this guy was. Knowing that they both felt far more at ease now was a relief.

Celeste and Marvin's niece was getting married the next day and Celeste had decided she most definitely could handle going with Laurent as her escort. She had been a little embarrassed to explain to him some of how she felt and her concerns. But his reception of all she said was good, open and accepting. It felt so okay to be open and honest with him.

Valerie did let her know though. "Daddy says he made a mistake marrying Carmine. Mom, if there is any chance you would want to get back with Daddy, let him know."

Celeste explained. "I will always love your Daddy, straight up. If your Daddy made a mistake, that damn sure don't have nothing to do with me, he needs to fix that all on his own."

Shannel came to her also. "Mom, Dad wants to talk to you. He is taking Carmine to the wedding but wants to talk to you first."

Celeste let her know. "Honey, I don't want to talk to him yet. If I go to the wedding and if he is there, okay… but we damn sure don't need to talk to each other prior, okay?"

*****

The wedding was a beautiful affair. Celeste wore a clingy, long red dress with a slit that fit her curves in a flattering way. Laurent had a charcoal suit that he set off with red and looked gorgeous to her. Judging from the glances from other women, they felt the same.

They made their entry, and lo and behold Marvin was nearby and came right up to them. Celeste was shocked to see Marvin had on blue jeans. She knew Marvin had a closet full of clothes, and to wear jeans at a white tux wedding was a total surprise to her.

She saw Carmine, in what she had heard was her classic black polyester pants and print top. Celeste internally rolled her eyes, hell this was maybe an indoor outfit, certainly not suited for this affair. Wow, I guess when one part of a couple was sort of downplayed... perhaps the other joined in, rather than step up.

Celeste could tell Marvin wanted a hug; she did not resist, nor did she embrace back, and he shook Laurent's hand introducing himself rather than allowing Celeste to do so. Her guess was he had tried to do a bone crusher handshake.

Carmine was damn near bopping over in their direction.

"If you'll excuse us," Celeste said, ignoring Carmine and walking towards the restrooms with Laurent.

"Thank you, for letting us get away from that," she told him quietly.

"Honey, we can do that all night long if that is what you want. You let me know what you want, what you need and that is what will happen." Laurent kissed her forehead, and let her go to the ladies room.

After the restroom break Celeste and Laurent went in another direction. They located family members and did introductions, then found seats before the actual wedding began.

It was a beautiful ceremony. Celeste certainly did not care to have Marvin and Carmine seated ahead of them, but there was plenty more interesting things to look at.

Her niece was gorgeous in her gown, and Celeste gave her a hug at the reception. She chatted with her parents and other's as well. When the music started she was ready to get up and dance, and did so with Laurent several times.

At one point, Laurent had gone to refresh drinks and Marvin swooped Celeste to the dance floor. She could feel Carmine's eyes on her, nothing discreet about it. She had seen Carmine sitting alone quite a bit with a lost dog look on her face, and actually for about a half a second felt sorry for her. The feeling quickly passed and Celeste was damn glad that she was in her own chair that night and not the one Carmine was sitting in. She had been there before, and it had not felt good.

When the song changed to a line dance, Marvin and Celeste stayed on the floor and Carmine damn near ran to get out there with them. Celeste let laughter go, finished the dance and joined her man who had his sexy smiling eyes focused on her.

"Hey handsome, are you having fun yet?" Celeste greeted, as she set down and accepted the drink he had gotten for her.

"It is a delight to watch you dance and have fun. I am indeed enjoying myself," Laurent replied.

After some more socializing, eating and dancing, picture taking and the cake was cut they bid farewell's and well wishes, and made the drive back to Portland.

Laurent drove them back. He handled the car like he handled everything else, very well. Celeste looked at him, marveling at what she had worried about. Over the course of the evening, having Laurent there, it had exceeded expectations, and went far beyond what she would have hoped. Celeste was so very grateful to have mostly avoided Carmine that evening.

There had been one point when they went to the food line, and Marvin suggested she and Laurent go in front of him, and that Celeste felt a little awkward. For one thing, Marvin was most definitely checking her out, ass and all.

Carmine was either being just silly assed, but more than likely trying to make a point as she kept hanging on Marvin, and calling him babe every chance she got. It was a little embarrassing and felt a bit offensive too.

Carmine obviously wanted to engage in a conversation with Celeste, but Celeste played deaf and blind and made sure that did not happen.

An hour and a half later, Celeste and Laurent were home and sat in the car a moment. Laurent would be heading back to Louisiana soon and it seemed to be on both of their minds. He turned to Celeste and let her know, "Celeste, these two weeks have flown by and there has not been one single moment where I did not want to be with you, spending this time, enjoying you and falling more in love with you too.

"Ummm, do weddings have you thinking commitments and romance?" Celeste shot back.

Laurent chuckled, took her chin and kissed her and said, "You have me thinking commitment and romance Celeste."

Celeste loved hearing these words, and was totally feeling this man. "So does that mean you're going to come visit me again soon or do you want to just go ahead and move here?"

"Visit soon and visit often. Move here is huge, but if I were going to ever move out of Louisiana, it would be to you," Laurent let her know.

It was nice to put the feelings out there and hear the words. It also brought reality real sharp. They lived in two different states, and he was heading home soon. But right now he was here, with her. Celeste was going to take this fine assed man into her home and make love to him, again and again, get all she could get before he left...

# Chapter 15

The morning Celeste took Laurent to the airport, she actually cried a little when he left and waved good-bye to her. It was so hard to believe this had happened for her, and so quickly. Celeste had anticipated staying quite single and was very set on not needing or even wanting a man. Her heart had been ripped apart, her life and dreams shredded, and she had been so done. She was not interested and not looking.

With Laurent gone she realized he had made an impact in her life so quickly. Laurent was in her heart, firmly planted. She had liked waking to him next to her, had liked going to sleep in his arms, and liked sharing their days together.

Since Laurent left, the house seemed to be too big and empty. Celeste made plans to get together with some of her ladies from her 'Kitchen Table' meeting to do water aerobics later in the week. She had also made shopping and lunch plans with Maria.

One thing she had learned from years with Marvin, being his wife and raising his kids, her life was full of family. That and work. When it all fell apart, she realized along the way she had not worked hard enough to nurture and maintain her female relationships. Well, everyone makes mistakes, she was trying to learn from hers and not repeat the same mistakes over again.

Acting as fillers, her kids let her know the grandbabies could come keep her company anytime. She had to laugh. Celeste did value her family, and loved this next generation running around. She thought every dang thing they did was cute.

Celeste had taken her phone number off her website once she left D.C., and saw no reason to put it back up or try to work and see any clients. Her cash was secure, her lifestyle comfortable. So this Portland Jewel was retired, short career as it was. She had managed to get $100,000 in money market accounts. Other than maintaining her home, keeping the lights on and eating, her expenses were not too much.

It just suddenly seemed that there was so much extra time on her hands, and not a day went by that Laurent did not cross her mind.

She tried real hard to not be calling him too much. Every time he called her, or she called him, the conversation was enjoyable. When they hung up she was always left feeling good.

Some days she wanted to talk to him several times throughout the day but held off, because she was an independent grown woman, and he a grown man, and she was not trying to come off all needy and acting thirsty and ish.

*****

Celeste found myrtle wood logs for sale, to make slabs off of or for other uses. Not cheap and even more expensive to ship. She did it anyway, and had the raw myrtle wood sent on its way to Laurent. She knew he would deeply value them, and create something beautiful with all that. She ran her hand across the book shelves he had made for her every day, and sat and admired them. They would bring her pleasure all of her days she knew.

Laurent sent her CD's of him singing, and even a song with her name in it dedicated to her. He wrote love letters, and she wrote love letters back. She went to Louisiana in October for a two week visit, and met so many family members of Laurent's. They made her feel welcome in their home.

That December Laurent came out to Oregon and spent the holidays with her. They enjoyed a trip to the mountains for snow play, and a night in the lodge with a roaring fire, watching the snow fall through the window. With the mountains and the coast so close to Portland, and with four solid seasons to enjoy, Laurent understood how Celeste could call this home and that she may never want to leave as well. Celeste had also told him so. With kids and grandkids, having just purchased a home, she loved to visit New Orleans but did not want to move there.

A few weeks spent together every couple months had their affair in full bloom. They both looked forward to and anticipated the visits, and took memories to draw on when they once again left each other.

It totaled three visits cross country for each of them in their first year of courtship. Celeste and Laurent enjoyed their time together, and their love and appreciation grew for one another. They did not feel the hurried need of youth to move in with each other quickly. There was not the need to start a family and be together every moment. Rather they honored each other their own lives and space, knowing each had their own families, and just taking time to enjoy one another and consider circumstances when they were apart.

In their second year of taking turns flying cross country the visits became more frequent and the stays became longer. Rather than every other month for two weeks, now they spent three weeks together and only a few weeks apart. Both of them realized they liked life better together.

Celeste really enjoyed all the visits to New Orleans, but also was glad to get back home, and knew that within weeks Laurent would join her in Portland. They spent more time together in their second year of courtship than they did apart, and it suited them both…

# Chapter 16

A cousin of Marvin's passed on, and Celeste attended the funeral. She sat with family and Carmine and Marvin did as well, just in another section. There came a point when forgiveness and apologies came out the preacher's mouth, encouraging those still alive to forgive, and to ask forgiveness where they needed to.

"I'm sorry if I have ever done anything to hurt you," Carmine spoke coming up behind Celeste.

Celeste felt vulnerable as it was; with tears for the loss of life of someone she actually did know and had love for. Celeste felt disadvantaged and caught off guard, but she spoke honestly.

"I've forgiven you, as much as I'm able to."

The fact that the amount was an absolute zero was left unspoken.

'Did this bitch really say if?' She thought. 'Was she out of her damn mind or what the hell? Was it humanly possible for her to really think she had never done anything that hurt Celeste? Wow.' This would bug Celeste for months to come. She had wished she were of a better head space at the time to really give this female a piece of her mind.

\*\*\*\*\*

She shared this story with her sister Yvette on the phone. Yvette told her, "What we sow, we reap. What is sent out to the Universe is what we receive back, and she will be receiving some big Karma soon."

Yvette's husband was finally declared dead, and all of his assets released. Yvette was now an extremely wealthy woman. She told Celeste she was in the process of relocating to San Diego, had found herself a wonderful cottage near the beach. Yvette's shop and apartment in New Orleans would be rented by one of the ladies that had done shifts there for so many years. It sounded like a good plan.

It was spring of 2005 and Laurent was due to arrive in Portland the next day for another three weeks. Celeste and Laurent had been doing the back and forth now for a few years.

When Laurent arrived, he surprised and delighted Celeste by getting on his knee in the traditional fashion and asking for her hand in marriage. He presented her with a gorgeous antique diamond ring.

It was an Edwardian cut 2.9 carat ring, in white gold with filigree. It was absolutely beautiful. Laurent put it on her finger, and she was surprised how perfect the fit was. He had been busy and chose well. She loved that it had come from Louisiana, and that he had chosen it himself and had it sized for her. It had been a long time since she had worn a ring on this finger. For so long, her ring finger had felt naked. She admired the ring's intricate beauty. If she had to choose something herself, Celeste did not think she would not choose such a large stone, but she certainly loved the design. *'The hell with it!'* It was large and gorgeous, and she loved it and would wear it proudly.

Laurent told her that after seven generations of family staying in New Orleans, he was going to make the big move and join her in Oregon. He was listing his home in Metairie and planned to have everything set and come back permanently in September. That would be the longest separation they had, but also the last. Celeste knew he had a great deal to do.

There would be a truckload to ship to Oregon. Just to get the house listed and sold would be a minimum of two months.

Celeste and Laurent threw an engagement party, and invited a houseful of people. They ordered a huge amount of Chinese food and Celeste cooked a few additional items as well to add to the spread. It was a nice May afternoon, and as usual people also wandered to the large outside areas to visit and smoke. She went ahead and put on a CD Laurent made for her and when the song came on he had wrote and sung with her name in it he came up to her. He took her in his arms to dance and sang it to her in person, with friends and family to witness.

That got a large round of applause when the song ended, and Celeste smiled looking around. All she saw were beams of smiles and love looking back at her.

Life had done a total 360, and it was a miraculous thing. She was so happy and felt very blessed.

Wedding plans became the topic and as so often happens, the guys ended outside and the gals inside with everyone almost talking at once. There were questions and excited suggestions. She wanted to get married as soon as Laurent returned in September, and decided to search the internet for venues and dates available. This would be, for both of them, their second marriages. Both had planned to only get married once, but for Laurent his wife had died. For Celeste, her marriage had died. She was certain though that this was it, this would be her final and permanent union.

Her first wedding had been small with no bridal party. It had been a beautiful little ceremony and she had worn the traditional gown and veil in ivory, with pearls and a sweetheart neckline. Celeste was thinking more along the lines of something form fitting in champagne this time around, perhaps with a small hat, or flowers in her hair.

She and Laurent had not discussed this, but as she talked with her girls, her vision became clearer and she was pretty sure Laurent would be down. And hey, if the man wanted tails and top hat, she would step up and be by his side complementing.

Once the gathering wound down and Laurent and Celeste were alone, they cuddled on the couch. She told him if he wanted top hat and tails it was cool. He laughed his deep sexy laugh and squeezed her and told her he would give it some thought.

They held each other and for the very first time made love without protection. Celeste had not had sex with anyone else since Laurent, and she believed the same for him. She realized that they could have waited until their wedding night, but at this moment Celeste wanted him totally inside of her with no barriers. She longed to feel as much of him as she could and to be as close as possible in their union. When they came, they looked into each other's eyes and she felt closer to him at that moment than she had with another human being in many, many years…

*****

When Laurent boarded the plane to Louisiana, he had only empty suitcases. He left what he had come with at Celeste's home that they would be sharing together. Celeste felt a strong desire to tell him not to go, just to stay and be with her from this day forward. She managed to work through the strong impulse to say these words out loud, and let the man leave so he could go handle his business and get back to her for their forever to begin…

# Chapter 17

Six days later it was said that Carmine was visiting a house in Vancouver by herself. It was she and Marvin's second real estate purchase, and it was a beautiful warm day. She had climbed a ladder and was checking on something apparently, when she disturbed an extremely large wasp nest that had not been seen from ground level.

No one was there to witness her fall or to see her landing hard. No one was there to hear the bones break in her back when she fell. No one was there to witness the wasps swarm her and begin their stinging. At some point she crawled to her handbag and it appeared she tried repeatedly to use an epinephrine auto injector (better known as an epi pen) on herself that would not inject, as there was bruising to indicate such and the malfunctioned epi pen lay nearby. She had a severe allergies to bee and wasp stings so she had always carried an epi pen, but on this day it proved useless to her as she met her end.

She was there for many hours prior to Marvin going by the house after he got off work. He found her lying on the side yard. Her stings were too many to count; it was believed that she continued to get stung mercilessly as she lay dying.

Celeste heard this story from one of her daughter's, who called to inform her. Valerie was distressed for her Dad that he had had to find Carmine this way and for what he had to deal with.

Celeste was quite sure it was not a pretty sight. But then again, when was death a pretty sight? She felt no sadness, no regret, why in the world would she? There would not even be words of condolences coming from her. Celeste was not about some fake bullshit on society expectations. She was not going to *'act'* like anything she was not. And she was not sorry or sad.

Celeste and Marvin's youngest daughter, Shannel, did not even go to the funeral, but did talk to her Dad a lot. She tried to talk Celeste into calling him.

"Mom, he really wants to talk to you, you spent all those years together! Can't you at least call him and talk with him at this time?" Shannel pleaded.

"Honey, there is nothing I can say to your Daddy that would even be nice right now. I'm not sorry, not sad. I do not feel bad for him, so what kind of talking do you expect me to do?" Celeste asked and then continued. "The same way you are not going to the funeral is the same way I do not even want to have a conversation about her, her dying, anything at all. I never have wanted any parts of her in my life or to discuss her, why the hell would I now?"

"Okay Mom, well I told him I would let you know...so I have," Shannel replied.

Celeste had over time lost interest in what her children's father did and did not do, and certainly wanted no parts in being involved in this in any kind of way.

When Marvin showed up at her door a few days after the funeral she was shocked. She had not even known he knew where she lived.

"Celeste, I'm sorry for dropping by. I tried to get messages for you to call me. I have something I have to give to you and something I really need to tell you," Marvin started out by saying the moment the front door was open. He stood back a few paces and Celeste, although shocked, decided to hear him out.

"Would you like to come in, or should we talk out here on the porch?" Celeste asked, and they decided to go on to the back deck. Celeste got them each an ice water while Marvin went to his trunk and brought out a box. They sat in lawn chairs on the deck. Celeste lit a cigarette, looked at the box and a terrible sense of certainty came over her. She knew exactly what it was. She had pictured it in her mind many times over the years. She had known it existed, and told Marvin so on many occasions.

"I'm so sorry Celeste, about so many things. I want you to know I never wanted anything bad to happen to Carmine, but I have always and always will love you more than I have ever felt about her. My very best day with her was not as good as my very worst day with you," Marvin said, not even realizing how each time he said Carmine's name, something in Celeste felt repulsed. She was torn between trying to have an open mind and being on bullshit alert status.

"Marvin...this box you have brought, did you open it?" Celeste nodded her head toward it and Marvin reached for it telling her, "I did. I found it in her closet. Oh my God, Celeste you had always said she had something like this. I honestly never believed that. I never wanted to believe it!"

"Don't open it in front of me; I don't want to see what is in there. It has to do with me, doesn't it?" Celeste asked, with a bit of panic and fear creeping into her voice.

"Yes, and I'm so, so sorry. Years ago, I asked her if she had ever done anything to harm you or bind me. She had told me about Dahlia wanting my shirt, but swore she never did anything to you! There are pictures of you; I think your hair, other things," Marvin trailed off.

Celeste cringed hearing Dahlia's name, a woman much older than them called the Black Dahlia, a self-proclaimed witch and astrologist. Celeste did not like her from their first meeting, did not trust her and that had never changed. It wasn't about a grudge; it was about keeping away negativity and bullshit.

"Okay, don't tell me anymore. Thank you for bringing it. I'll figure out how to be rid of it," Celeste said looking hard at Marvin, thinking he looked scared she asked "Are you okay? Have you felt bad energy or anything?"

Marvin sat the box back down and put his head in his hands. He took a long breath and then replied, "Truth is Celeste I have felt much freer since Carmine died. It was subtle but real, like something has been lifted. When I found this box I thought it was like something from a horror movie. Touching it feels terrible, and I wanted to burn it or throw it away. You told me it existed for so long, and because a part of you is in it, I knew the right thing to do would be to bring it to you. I need to apologize. I'm so very sorry to have not believed you, and for so many other things. Marrying her was a mistake. I knew it from day one, I am truly free now, and I love you. I always have."

"I have heard that before, but yet you stayed married to her. You broke my heart, but it has been healed. With love Marvin, I found love, and I'm getting married again. Your timing sucks. It is pretty unfair to come here now and lay all this out." Celeste felt herself getting emotional having to say these words.

"I know, and I'm glad for you. I hope he is good to you and good for you. I love you and I just wanted to tell you how I felt. If you have any doubt about this other guy, then please consider waiting and give us another chance." Marvin tried to hold her hands; Celeste pulled away and stood up, going back into the house.

"We are marrying in September. He has never made me cry, has never lied to me, and has never cheated on me. I won't betray him by even having this conversation," Celeste spoke raised her voice with these words.

"That you know of," Marvin said, "He hasn't lied to you or cheated on you that you know of. But then, how would you?"

Celeste looked at him hurt and shocked, these words felt cruel, and any inkling of pity she had felt for Marvin vanished just that quickly. She let him know, "I think you better go now."

"Celeste, I'm sorry, I shouldn't have said that. Maybe I'm jealous. This is not how I wanted things to end. I had hoped you would show me your house, I would really like to have your number."

"I have your number. I'll think about it. Maybe see the house another time. Thanks for bringing the box and all." Celeste walked him to the door, he went in for an embrace but she felt like if she gave into it she would cry, maybe even fall apart, so she held him at bay and told him goodbye. When she shut the door, she cried and slid down the wall. Sitting on the floor with her head in her hands Celeste loudly shed more tears...

# Chapter 18

Celeste called Yvette and told her what had happened. Yvette was concerned, but always level headed with a plan and gave her solid instructions and advice.

"Okay girl. Leave the box on the deck and do not open it. Your eyes do not need the memory, nor your mind. There probably is not much to it now, but I am going to gather some things and overnight them to you with instructions. In the meantime, I want you to quickly pack a bag and get out of there for the night," she continued. "Stay with one of your kids or get a hotel room but do not sleep there. This negative energy has come through your door, went through your home and is now present. I want you to properly rid yourself of this ugly evil before you sleep there again. We are vulnerable in our sleep. Give me Marvin's address too, I want to send him something to take care of the space he shared with her and the place she had this box hidden. He may not believe in all this, or do it, but I need to send it to him anyway."

"Thank you sister. I love you so much Yvette. Let me get on out of here then," Celeste told her and hung up after giving her Marvin's address, which she found while on the phone using the internet.

Celeste packed a small bag and her computer. She packed her JR Ward book and went to a nearby hotel with a pool.

She spent her evening securing her venue for her wedding. Hood River Stone Hedge looked fabulous. Early September should be great weather, and she booked it for the 10th. She scheduled a visit for the upcoming week, when she could walk the grounds and sit down with someone to do additional planning and sign papers.

Looking online there were some gorgeous dresses; she had picked out an Alex Evenings and an Adriana Papell she wanted to try on.

She wished Laurent would use the internet so he could check them out too. When she called him, he told her whatever she wanted would be fine and he would complement the color. Laurent had decided to have Michael and Kenny Ray be best men, and Celeste decided to have Valerie and Shannel be her bridesmaids. When Marvin and Carmine married, none of the kids even got invited, let alone were involved in their wedding. Well, at hers they would be present and participating.

Celeste also told Laurent about Marvin's visit and how that had all played out. He listened to her, and supported whatever her mind or heart told her to do. He also said, "Celeste, the man was out of his mind to let you go so I am sure he is feeling something about now. Invite him to the wedding if you want!" He gave her his sexy laugh and let her know, "I'm marrying you and we are spending the rest of our lives together. Nothing and nobody will come between us. I know this deep into my soul and I'm not worried about your ex or anybody else."

"I love you baby," Celeste told him, before they hung up and she went back to the computer.

She decided to give her girl's free reign on their dresses. She sent them both emails and included pictures of the two gowns she herself was considering, so they could get started. She let them know the date, and left it up to them to compare notes and decide.

Next, she set about ordering invitations. It was cool to do all this online. Celeste loved her computer. She looked over floral arrangements too, but figured she had time for that. Her mind was full of plans and thoughts about the big day.

She took a swim and a shower, and called it a night with her Black Dagger book from the JR Ward series she was totally into.

The next day she went home to a package waiting on her steps. She had already gotten an email from Yvette explaining, so opened the package, read again the instructions and set about lighting the variety of herbs that had been sent and candles. She said prayers, and went through the rituals set out for her.

Celeste believed strongly in prayer, and in sending out the positive energy to have it returned. In this case, it was about removing any negative energy or evil power, and then replacing it. She would surround herself with only good, and only with what God would bless and honor.

Ashes to ashes and dust to dust, she rid any trace of what had been done to and against her. Carmine was gone, and now so was any possibility of a hold or influence on her.

As far as Marvin went, she did not know. She had tried in years past to tell him about

Carmine. Now he had proof, but what he would do, if anything, was unknown to her and not within her power. Any power Celeste had ever had over Marvin was with love, commitment and family, and that had not been enough to have and to hold to keep it all together. Now it had no value or pull on him...

# Chapter 19

Wedding plans kept Celeste busy and excited. June came and went. In July, Yvette called her, having just moved out of New Orleans.

"Hi, Celeste," Yvette exclaimed. "I'm so excited about your wedding," She started off.

"Yvette, I'm so glad I drove through Louisiana and hooked up with you those days a few years back. That is when I met Laurent, and it has developed into a beautiful thing. No, you know what? It started as a beautiful thing. Now we're going to make it permanent. I can't wait for him to get all his affairs in order and get back here."

"That's why I'm calling Sis. I did a reading just to see how everything aligned and Laurent really needs to come out to Oregon in July. Tell him to get everything wrapped up and get out to you," Yvette explained.

"What do you mean? Is something going to happen if he isn't here with me?" Celeste ventured.

"I don't know what will or will not happen, just that the cards show he should travel in July, not August or September which is his current plan, right?"

"Umm yeah, that is his current plan. Well, I will pray on it and pass this on to him. I would love him to come out now," Celeste chuckled.

After they hung up she called Laurent. He said he would come as soon as he could. His house had interested a few potential buyers and he was in the process of giving away what was not going to come with him. Celeste talked about flying down to drive out to Oregon with him. She wasn't too worried about her sister saying he should come in July. It was a possibility, and Yvette did not seem insistent or worried really.

July passed and August came. Laurent was closing on the house the last week of August, and would come directly after. Everything was ready and Celeste was counting the days.

*****

On Wednesday, August 24th a Tropical Depression hit Florida and was upgraded to a Tropical Storm and they named it Katrina. It was hurricane season, and this was pretty common really. A close eye would be kept, but that too was standard issue. The hurricanes went through the alphabet getting their names. So K followed, many was number nine of that year.

On Thursday, The 25th of August, winds hit 75 MPH. The storm hit north of Miami causing fatalities, and over a million people were without power. Now the storm was at a category 1.

On Friday, August 25th Hurricane Katrina became a category 2 and that morning fear for New Orleans came, since so much of the city is below sea level. Winds were now at 100 MPH. Reports were that Katrina will turn and head for Mississippi and Louisiana.

Celeste called Laurent. "Laurent I want you to leave there, get out before the storm hits. Go back later."

He replied, "Cheri, I have ridden out many storms, and heard so many warnings over the years. Baby, if the Hurricane does hit hard, I would rather be here to help people. I will need to check on folks. I got a boat, I got supplies, I been through this many times."

They talked a little while longer. Celeste tried to feel calm, and Laurent sounded calm. Perhaps she was worried over nothing. The news has a way of exaggerating sometimes. Heck, a little snow or ice in Portland, and the news would try to run winter storm coverage all day long.

Saturday, August 27th, Hurricane Katrina is now category 3 with winds at 115 Mph. St. Tammany Parish was ordered to mandatory evacuate. That was where Big Mama was, on the North Shore in Mandeville. Celeste called for a long time before someone finally answered at Big Mama's. She was told family was trying to get Big Mama to go.

The Mayor said he would stick with the City's evacuation plan, and not order a mandatory evacuation until thirty hours prior to landfall. Celeste was confused. She had just seen different information on the TV. She gave her love and hung up. She prayed and was glad there was family there figuring out a plan and what was in the best interest. She wasn't there and had to trust that folks knew what they needed to do.

She saw that Jefferson Parish was on a volunteer evacuation, which was where Metairie was located and where Laurent was. She tried calling him, and got no answer. Celeste continued watching the television coverage, the Mayor cautioning those that planned to stay to gather supplies, water and food.

Celeste continued to leave the television on throughout the day. Even when she was not sitting down and watching she could hear the coverage. Celeste kept finding herself drawn back to the television and she watched as drivers were gridlocked on all roads out of town, and knew there was no way everyone would get out. For so many people, where would they go to? There were so many more with no cars to leave, even if they had wanted to and had a place to go.

The scariest fear was an actual direct hit.

Sunday, August 28th. Hurricane Katrina was a category 5 with wind's at 160 MPH. It was coming towards the mouth of the Mississippi River. It was actually going to hit with a projected water storm surge of 18-22 feet, in some areas 28 feet. It was really going to hit, and hit hard.

Celeste was horrified as one projection after another was made, talking about most of the city not being habitable for weeks. They would be with no power for that long, and covered in water. A mandatory evacuation was issued. Roads were still packed. Celeste called Laurent and called Big Mama, with no answer at either place and watched with panic. She was looking at the cars on the news, looking at the area, the people, trying to see if she saw someone she knew.

The Superdome was opened for emergency evacuation. The National Guard brought truckloads of water and food, to feed fifteen thousand people for three days. By the evening, there were thirty thousand people at the Superdome.

Monday, August 29th, no longer categorized a 5, now Katrina is listed as a category 4 briefly and the wind has slowed from 160 to 145 MPH. The storms eye passed eastern New Orleans. It looks like the city avoided a direct hit.

Katrina did hit landfall at 127 MPH in The Grand Isle area.

Then, the water began to break, and come over the levees. The wind rips a piece off the Superdome roof. The power goes out, flood waters continue to rise. Windows are blown out, roofs are ripped off. Interstate 10 is shut down, with over forty percent damage to the bridge over Lake Pontchartrain. Phone service and electricity are gone in most of the area, and water kept coming over the levees. The lootings begin. People have lost their minds.

Valerie came and set with Celeste for long extended periods of time to watch the horror unfold. It looked like a war zone, belonging somewhere far removed from civilization. They both cried seeing people trapped, seeing bodies floating, a dead woman in a wheelchair covered with a sheet outside of the Dome.

No electricity, no lights, no air conditioning. No phone service, and no food or water.

Buses were ordered to come and remove people, but they were delayed in arriving. Boats set unused, but they were all ready to go out and try to rescue people.

Celeste and Valerie cried, it had been days already. Valerie tried to remind and make sure Celeste ate. Nerves on edge, worry and sadness consumed them both. There were many others across the country that had their T.V. turned to this ongoing coverage.

There was a lot of belief that not enough was done in time. President Bush was an embarrassment, but that was not exactly new news.

Tuesday, August 30th. The Army Corps of Engineers tried to plug one of the levees and it did not hold, the flooding continued. Looting continued. Eighty percent of the area was flooded.

The situation was horrible. People were seen doing whatever they wanted on the television. Even police officers were seen looting. Guns were stolen, so now armed people roamed taking whatever they could and doing whatever they wanted. Stories of rape and deprivation at the Superdome and surrounding areas were being told.

This was the worse real life thing Celeste had ever witnessed with her own eyes. She sat watching it all unfold. She saw trucks overturned, cars floating, people floating, and roofs caved in with people hanging on for dear life.

Wednesday, August 31st. Governor Blanco and President Bush gave Guardsmen the authority to shoot to kill if need be, after a rescue helicopter was shot at. Amongst their job duties was to put an end to the looting, and gain control over citizens. It was a tense and horrible time.

They arrived in large numbers and came heavily armed to a mob of people needing help, thirsty, hungry and scared. The Guardsmen had dropped water and food, and asked people to share. It was controlled chaos.

When Celeste watched three star Lieutenant General Russel Honore' take control on the Guardsmen, ordering them to lower their M-16s, she felt such gladness for his control and good sense. He hollered out to the Guardsmen for all to hear, "This is not Baghdad! These are American citizens! These are American Citizens!"

Finally something that made sense, someone in charge that recognized.

Busloads of people were taken to the Houston Superdome, but as people began to board buses they were not told where they were going. Families were separated. Officials were trying to take priorities first. People were scared to go and scared to stay. It was devastating to watch this; Celeste kept thinking, *'can't it be handled better.'*

Her tears flowed as she witnessed elders going one place, and the younger generation on a completely different bus. Would they find each other? How long would it take? Were these people ever going to be able to come back? And, what would they come back to? The city was in ruins and it wasn't over yet...

# Chapter 20

September 1st. There were still no calls from anyone from Louisiana. Celeste and Laurent's wedding was planned and scheduled for September 10th. It was decided that Maria and Celeste's daughters would come over with her daughter in law Annabella to help. They would help Celeste to call everyone to cancel the wedding, since calls to Louisiana going unanswered. The girls also called the venue, the florist and all else involved and needing to know.

Celeste was so grateful for the help and the support. To hell with a wedding, she wanted a husband. She wanted her man to show up safe. She knew not everyone was out yet, he could still be alright. Celeste was certain that Laurent knew her phone number by heart. She had given her number to a second cousin at Big Mama's, but had no idea if they were separated or what had happened.

There were some buses that had made it out, so lists were being compiled. Celeste knew so many of these people moved by bus were separated not only from home and what was familiar, but from family as well. Some for the very first time in their lives...

Four hundred and seventy five Guardsman trucks were on their way with supplies, there were still tens of thousands of people stuck in New Orleans and the surrounding areas.

Hospitals began to try and evacuate, food, water and ice was getting delivered. All police on search and rescue missions were ordered to stop, and they had enforced a curfew. The looting and mayhem continued. There were estimates on the body count being in the thousands.

The suburb of Gretna turned back those fleeing from New Orleans over the bridge by gunpoint. Accusations of racism were everywhere. The Chief of Police of Gretna said that was not the case, but that their city was on lockdown, and not equipped to handle the evacuees from New Orleans.

The work on pumping away water, and trying to close the levees' continued.

Bush wanted to issue a federal takeover. The talks went on all night and were finally refused by Governor Blanco. He thought that it would be compared to a federal declaration of martial law.

By September 4th, the New Orleans Superdome was finally completely cleared. Almost ten thousand people from hospitals had been moved. The Coast Guard air operations had rescued over twelve hundred people, and the USGC helicopters saved over a thousand more from roof tops.

Efforts continued in the days that followed. A lot of hold outs did not want to leave New Orleans, but conditions were hazardous. Talks of disease, E coli, and other illnesses were made between trying to persuade and trying to force people to leave their homes.

Sean Penn, the actor went to New Orleans, because he could not stand to watch from home and not help. Support came from many celebrities, and would continue for many years. Kanye West said the president didn't like black people, telethons were done, and awareness and money were raised.

On September 9th, media was asked to not report on the recovery of dead bodies. CNN filed a suit to not be restricted.

September 10th came. The day that once would have been her wedding. Celeste twirled the ring on her finger, having shed so many tears, her skin felt tight. She had somehow lost twelve pounds and her eyes were so tired. Her body so tired and her mind so tired. Restless sleep had evaded her for weeks now. This was what true powerlessness felt like.

September 19th evacuees were being allowed to come back, but then turned away again because Hurricane Rita was on her way.

October 1st. 1.5 million people were evacuated from Louisiana. Roughly, 1 million had applied for hurricane-related federal aid. Thirty thousand were in out-of-state shelters, forty-six thousand and four hundred were in state shelters and over ten thousand were known dead.

Still, there was no word from Laurent. At this point, Celeste felt certain there would not be. The realization had come and had to be acknowledged, even if she was still unable to accept. She had been checking online lists of people, named and unknown.

Craigslist had started a new category so that Hurricane Katrina victims could post, as well as those offering help. There was also another section that was interactive with exchanging of information and directing those seeking it.

Celeste felt pissed that Laurent had not ever shown a lick of interest to ever even get on the computer. He had had zero desire to know what information could be found and what could be accomplished on the internet. He had no damn email address and she was mad about it, mad that a possibility to communicate did not exist.

She hoped that he was okay somewhere, maybe he had been injured, maybe he didn't know who he was, had suffered a terrible shock.

As October continued, homes were searched in the New Orleans area, and large X's put on the door to show the inside had been searched. Sometimes numbers added, to indicate bodies were found inside. Over six thousand people were still missing.

The name Laurent Almonester appeared on the missing person list towards the end of October. Celeste was devastated to see it. If he were dead she wanted to know, to have this acknowledged. If he were alive she wanted to know, to go to him.

She called, "Sis, Laurent's name is on the missing persons list from Katrina."

"Oh Celeste, honey, I'm so sorry. I was hoping for a different outcome," Yvette sadly responded.

"Do you feel anything, do you have any certainty?" Celeste asked her sister. She had called and asked the same before.

"I don't, I really don't. If I did, I would have called you. I try to tap in and there is a fog, a void. I just am uncertain if he is dead and has not transferred to a new existence, or if he is alive but somehow lost from himself," Yvette sighed and then continued. "Pray sis. Keep praying for clarity. I am certain you will be with him again, I just don't know if it will be in Earthly form."

"Thank you honey. I really appreciate that. I think I need to go to New Orleans," Celeste said the words out loud that had been playing through her mind since the beginning of this disaster. The same words she had repeated to everyone she talked with.

"It's a mess down there, where would you stay? How could you even get around?" Yvette was not feeling this idea at all. "People are looking hard, they have resources, and what can you do? Even volunteers are sleeping in tents."

"Oh gosh, that is what everyone keeps saying. I feel so helpless just sitting here, in comfort. I want to find Laurent. I want to be with him." Celeste almost sobbed the words out and tears were running down her cheeks.

"I know you do. Sometimes we truly are helpless, powerless. You cannot change what is. Have faith. Don't go down there and see the horror and walk amongst it, how in the world would that help anything?" Yvette was so set on it being a bad idea.

Celeste could hear the irritation creep into her sister's voice. She knew there was no point in continuing to talk about it. It felt like no one supported what she wanted to do, and because Celeste knew she was not thinking straight she accepted that everyone else was right.

Her heart though, her heart wanted her to go anyway.

Celeste did some searching and made some phone calls. It appeared most hotels were renovating and housing recovery workers. It was like a war zone, third world living in the United States. The heartbreak was too immense, and she considered her options. She prayed, asking God for direction and signs, maybe some answers, and she tried very hard to clear her mind. She needed to breathe slowly and in a cleansing manner.

Celeste wanted desperately to rid herself of her own fears and the horrible images she kept seeing on the television. Those images were then replaying over and over in her mind. In her own mind too, she added to the images and saw entire scenarios. Walked the ruined streets, saw the torn homes, the rubble of what was people's lives lying about.

Things were such a terrible mess, and Celeste felt she could do very little by trying to go herself, and trying to find accommodations. Resources were stretched as it was for the people there, trying to rebuild and help and survive…

# Chapter 21

Celeste got herself a ticket to go see Steel Pulse at the Roseland. She and Marvin had seen them in Seattle years ago, and another time in Portland. They were her favorite Reggae band from the first time she had ever heard them, and remained so. She was up in the balcony getting her jam on, the floor below filling with people. There was a huge pulsating crowd and marijuana smoke streamed up to the balcony, as joints were passed in several parts of the room.

Security came and removed some people a few times, and folks were even throwing joints on stage. Celeste had her full groove going when she felt a presence next to her and turned to see Marvin had maneuvered to being body to body beside her. She had not even known he was there.

Last she knew an adorable little Asian gal and her boyfriend had been there. The lady getting more friendly and touchy feely as the night wore on and her alcohol consumption continued. Celeste was in mid jam, singing, smiling, moving her body and Marvin slid right in and joined with her. It did not slow Celeste down, and after "True Democracy" finished they clapped loudly, and then embraced each other. It was a natural response.

    Celeste had spent so many years with this man and had loved him always. She loved him even when she hated his choices and his actions. The fact they had both come solo and were here next to each other was a feel good, actually the best Celeste had felt since Katrina.

    When Steel Pulse left the stage and then got clapped and hollered back on, the crowd was on full alert and this magnificent band hit the stage and broke into "Rally Round." It was on then and the whole place responded.

    There were arms swaying... voices joining in...and bodies were in movement. The applause was thunderous. They played a few more songs after that to close out the show. Celeste was totally satisfied, and she and Marvin began to make their way down the stairs and out into the fresh air that waited.

"Fantastic show!" Celeste shouted, as she moved away from the door to light a cigarette.

"It was. And fancy meeting you here." Marvin grinned at her.

"You too. Amazing you even saw me in that crowd," Celeste remarked laughing.

"I could never be anywhere with you present and not know. I saw you from across the room, my total senses felt you and then my eyes found you and I could not look away." Marvin rubbed her hand.

"Sweet talker, always so smooth." Celeste squeezed his hand in response.

"I am telling you the truth woman. Can I walk you to your car? Or better yet, want to go eat?" he asked.

"I'm parked up the block on Couch. Tell you the truth I am hungry, but we should take both cars, yes?" Even as she spoke these words, which were honest and how she felt, there was also a bit of a warning bell, a small tinkling deep inside of her. Was this the wisest thing to do? What was she really getting herself into? Where would this lead? And what would happen? 'Damn girl, it's just a meal,' she told herself; 'you have had thousands of meals with this man.'

When they got to Celeste's car, Marvin asked where she wanted to go. She chose a spot pretty close at Third and Morrison. "How about Le Bistro Montage? ...Cajun food? A little cool hideaway spot not far?"

"Fantastic, see you there," he said as he closed her door and waited for her to start her car up.

Celeste drove over the Burnside Bridge, made a few turns and went to park, and she just had to laugh that Marvin was already there parking his car. "How does he do that?" She questioned out loud with a smile on her face. This man always seemed to be able to locate her and also get where she was going quicker than she could.

"Hey you," Celeste laughed as she got out of her car and walked over to join Marvin. They entered the spot with Marvin holding the door open and were seated. They were exchanging smiles and feeling comfortable. Both of them chose red beans and rice with cornbread, and it was fantastic. The conversation was so easy; they talked about the evening, their past Steel Pulse shows, the food and the kids.

"How about a dessert?" Marvin asked, looking over the dessert menu. He chose Mississippi mud pie and Celeste ordered the rum raisin bread pudding with coffee. Marvin never drank coffee, he said it hyped him up, this man who had done immeasurable amounts of cocaine could not handle a cup of coffee. Celeste made a joke about it and they talked some about their recovery and what each did to stay clean and drug free.

"Marvin, I'm really so glad you have been able to live drug free. It is great to see you clean, I am very happy for you."

"Celeste, I am too. Thank you. I appreciate your saying that. I wish I would have stopped earlier. Not had to lose you as my wife, and lose our home. Have I ever told you how sorry I feel about that?"

"You are now, and I appreciate it. So how are you these days, living alone again?" Celeste asked.

"What you saying, you want to live with me?" Marvin joked, as Celeste shook her head and told him "Never mind." They both laughed.

Then he got very serious. "Celeste, I don't even know what to say to you. I know you were engaged, should be married by now. I'm so sorry that Laurent is missing. I know this is hard on you and I wish it were different. No matter what has ever happened with us I always want for you to be happy."

Celeste felt a rush of emotion. Tears could stream so easily, she took a very deep breath as Marvin held her hand.

Celeste spoke slowly and carefully, "Marvin, thank you. I know that. It means a lot."

He nodded, and rubbed her hand gently as she took another deep breath.

She sighed and went on, "Not knowing what's happening that is so hard. It hurts terribly."

Marvin scooted closer and took her in his arms. He kissed her head, rubbed her back and held her as he murmured sweet comfort. Then he took his fingers to her chin and raised her face to him. Quietly, with both his words and his eyes he told her.

"Let me comfort you tonight. Let the past be gone. Just tonight Celeste, let me hold you and love you for all the years we were together. For all the pain I put you through and the pain you're in now. Let me take that away and love and comfort you tonight."

Celeste put her arms around this man and their lips touched gently and sweetly. These kisses were indeed a comfort, and she felt herself not only agreeing, but wanting this. Wanting this man to hold her, to make love to him and find the blissful release she needed. Sorrow, loneliness, fear and grief had been a part of her life daily for over two months and tonight she decided to let it all go. Tonight, she would have this man in her bed. She would hold him and find comfort and security. There would be the release of pain and the absence of loneliness.

*****

Marvin entered her bed, and then he entered her mind and her body, and even her heart. They both enjoyed the familiarity that their coupling brought. They felt at ease with the passion unleashed, and the sweet release that followed. Not once, but twice. Back to back, as if they were years younger than what they were. And then they lay together. Celeste did not need words and hoped Marvin would not speak any that would take away from this moment. He did not, instead he kissed her head, stroked her back all the way down to her backside, and Celeste felt her body hunger for more.

He slipped his fingers expertly to her sweet spot and began movement that she could not help but join. As she began to come once more, he pulled her close and entered her from the side while still stroking her clitoris. It was a good thing he had a strong grip on her because the intense orgasm had her bucking and it was impossible for her to hold herself in place. As he continued to fuck her throughout her orgasm, she reached a heightened level of pleasure and squirted her juices all over this man as she called his name. He responded, thrusting into her vagina, giving her every drop of his cum, both of them left with shuddering aftershocks.

Sleep followed, and in the morning Marvin woke first. He turned on the coffee and then showered. Celeste awoke, put a thin robe over her naked body.

Pouring herself a cup of coffee, she looked out the window. Fall was making its appearance. She sat outside with her cup, lit a cigarette and tried to ask herself if at that very moment she felt any regrets about her night with Marvin. Celeste decided, no. Regret and guilt would serve no purpose. She and Marvin had come together, shared a good evening and it was done.

Marvin joined her on the deck dressed and Celeste could feel that he was ready to go. She did not know if he was struggling with any mixed feelings or not.

"Hey Celeste, good morning. You're looking beautiful," he told her.

"Umm, thank you. It has been a long time since we saw each other first thing in the morning. You have an advantage, looking real fresh from a shower." She replied.

"I love your shower too! It is good to see you first thing in the morning. I would like to see you much more than we have, I really would. Hope we can?" He formed these last words in a question, and Celeste agreed. She then walked him to the door, as he let her know he had places to go and things to do.

After she shut the door, she felt a little bit of a nag. She had known when he came outside that he would be leaving soon, had sensed his need to go.

Sure, okay the man had things to do, but somehow it felt not very good to her. They had history. That was for sure.

Maybe too much history, too many broken promises, unfaithful behavior, lies and bullshit to even consider moving forward in any kind of way.

Still, she wasn't going to lie to herself, the sex was good. Their evening was good. Men seemed to be able to just leave it at that more so than women. Well, at least not this woman...

# Chapter 22

Celeste went and located a tent, bought a new air mattress with an automatic pump and packed lightly in a carry on. The first week of November, she flew to Baton Rouge. Then picked up a rental car and drove towards New Orleans.

After her night with Marvin, she reached a decision to go to Louisiana. Even if it were a bad idea, even if absolutely no one she knew thought she should. It was one of those moments in life when something just must be done. For her, she had to do this. It simply did not matter what anyone else thought. Celeste had to go to Metairie; she had to try to get to Laurent's home. She had to see with her own eyes first hand.

The devastation was everywhere. Seventy five percent of the area had been under water. There had been a mandatory evacuation and no residents were allowed back for over two weeks. As water was removed, structural damages continued. So much of the area was not livable, but yet families were in yards to sleep, and doing what they could to repair.

There were entire camps of residents, as well as those that came to try and help. In one area it looked like little Mexico. Hard working travelers had come, and there was certainly enough to do. Yet, frustrations were voiced on bullshit permits needed and regulations for those working. Police were out to enforce and to stop what looked to Celeste like actual progress.

She herself was pulled over and asked her business. Celeste showed ID and car rental information and told the officer.

"My fiancé has been missing; I want to see his house up the road."

She was shocked when the cop informed her.

"That is not possible. Every house has been checked, there are no bodies. No one is allowed to go inside any of these homes."

"Why?" She pleaded, feeling desperate and determined not to just be blown off.

"Trespassing for one ma'am, it's not your property. In addition, it's dangerous. Debris is down in the road and homes are not stable. We got enough folks hurt, and resources are spread thin enough. Going to have to insist you leave the area. Go back home. There is nothing for you to do here."

"Well, just the same I'd like to continue down the road to see anyway, even if there is nothing I can do," Celeste replied, she was feeling defensive and angry.

The police officer said something into his radio and told her to get out of the car. She was shocked when she was handcuffed and put in the back of the cruiser.

The jail was too water damaged to have anyone held there, so instead Celeste was taken to Orleans Parish Prison. She sat in an eight foot by twelve foot cell with a toilet and a large water jug with cups. One bench lined each side of the two walls.

Women were laying on the floor. They also sat on the floor as well and on benches. Celeste herself sat on the floor until a space on a bench became available, and then sat there for four days and four nights. At one point there were twenty seven women in this holding cell. She looked around at the women, for the most part black. The only three women that were white were arrested trying to help clean up homes and property that they were told they were not authorized to do.

There was water damage that could be seen on the walls, the line went over four feet high in this room. One woman was removed for banging her head and causing herself to bleed. Another was removed for having a fit and knocking over the water cooler.

A few doors down there appeared to be a mentally challenged white man babbling to himself. A disturbed black man was brought in and put into the room with him, and they began to fight, throwing punches and their bodies. Guards on duty laughed, and Celeste believed it had been intentional just for amusement. When the men were brought out they were bloodied.

On her second day there Celeste was removed from the holding cell and taken to be photographed and fingerprinted. She was asked health questions, about HIV and diabetes and other conditions. She was told there would be a hearing and if there was a bail, it would be set at that time. She asked for a telephone call and was told someone would let her do that later. And then she was returned to the holding cell.

It felt like she was in hell. The women seemed shell shocked; they had all been through so damn much and now in here held like animals. The charges were incredulous as she listened to their stories.

One woman said she never got a court notice, and Celeste believed her. Mail was not running normally, many places were unable to get mail, there was no one there. There was still water and damage in so any areas, maybe even a door gone that had once had a mail slot, or the whole damn mailbox itself gone. To be held in jail for not responding to a court notice seemed Ludacris under the circumstances.

Another was hauled in for vagrancy; she had lost all of her ID and had no home. Another brought in for imposed curfew violation. The ninth ward was on shut down, and no one was to leave or enter once evening came. It seemed that so many of the women Celeste encountered and talked to were there basically as a direct result of the storm.

The sheer stupidity involved in all these women being held was insane. What a waste, and the guards themselves some seemed not quite right. Everyone had been affected by the hurricane. Even police officers had been called on for their behavior during the storm. One officer that was transporting prisoners during Katrina let the whole van full of prisoners go. He said he was not going to lock up men in a flooding jail and went to go see about his own family.

Story after story was told to Celeste. Stories of people who had been in jail dying. Stories from these women that now had no home, or whose family was misplaced, or whose life had fallen apart through the devastation. And they sat in this room, the process insanely slow. They were given bologna sandwiches three times a day. That was it, just bologna and bread. Sometimes, the bologna had a purple or green tinge to it.

Celeste would hear the clanging of doors, see officers and guardsmen bringing in new prisoners. Many more men than women and almost all of them were black. It seemed the men got processed faster than the women. There were more male guards than female. Perhaps that was why.

On the fourth day, finally Celeste was brought out of the holding cell. This was when she was taken to another room where the water marks from Katrina raged higher than standing height. Her mind was in a fog. *'How was that possible?'* she wondered. The females with her were lined into one row. There were seven rows, and across from them to the side probably seven rows of men. The females were told to keep their heads straight and their mouths shut.

One by one they got called forward, in front of everyone else. It was a surreal experience. The judge was not even in the room. A 25 inch television was there in his place. He spoke to them that way. The bailiff brought Celeste forward and told her she was charged with disobedience to a police officer and trespassing. Celeste was terrified. Did not know if she should plead guilty and hope she would get time served and released. She was afraid to plead not guilty and have to stay in this horrible place until trial.

The judge straight up asked her if she wanted bail and a trial. Yes! "Yes your honor." Celeste croaked out. Bail was set at $2,500 and a court date set for a month from then.

Celeste was told to sit back down, and she listened to each woman go up and go through their process, and then they were herded back to the holding area.

A few women were taken to get further processed in, to be given jail clothes and moved to a dorm setting.

One was set aside to begin her release process. Celeste and two others were told they could make a phone call and see about bail. When Celeste's turn came, she gave her daughter's phone number. It was dialed and the guard asked for Valerie. Then she said, "This call is from Parish Prison, an inmate Celeste Lacoste wishes to speak with you, will you take this call?" The phone was then handed to Celeste.

The relief of hearing her daughter's voice brought a flood of emotion in Celeste, and she felt tears come to her. "Oh Mom, I am so glad to hear from you. I been calling hospitals and the jail for days! They act like they didn't even know they had you until two days ago! Why are you in a prison?"

"The jail is not able to have prisoners because of damage, so people are being housed here in Parish Prison. This has been pretty bad. I just got a bail set though, now I need to figure out how to get out. I hope I can use my bank card." Celeste said. Her voice, she knew was unstable but she could just not put the words out without the emotion too.

"You can't Mom, we already checked. Dad flew down today. He is already there trying to get it paid and get you out, but he had to go get cash." Valerie sounded upset, no doubt figuring things out on her end had been worrisome and frustrating too.

*'Your Dad is here? To get me?'* The thought had not even entered Celeste's mind. She was truly surprised, and instantly relieved.

"Yes. Mama we been so worried, all of us have been trying to figure things out. He is there right now. You're getting out. Call me when you do, it's going to be okay. Alright? I love you."

"Yes, okay. Yes baby. Thank you. Good bye, talk to you soon." Celeste handed the phone back to the guard, and told her someone was already here paying her bail.

The guard said. "Okay, we'll check on that in a moment when phone calls are done. You can sit back down there."

The next part of the process took close to an hour. Celeste signed papers, got her purse and two doors were opened to let her out into a small and crowded area where people waited for loved ones. There were three guards at desks behind bullet proof glass, processing people out Celeste assumed.

Marvin embraced her, and Celeste felt horrible to have him this close. She had sat in her same clothes for four days in an overcrowded tiny room. She felt unclean and unwell. Marvin seemed not to notice or care. He hugged her and said. "Let's get you out of here."

As soon as they got outside Celeste stopped. Got in her purse and lit a cigarette. "I suppose this would have been a real good time to stop. But, today is not the day. Marvin that was the worse place I have ever been."

She looked at this man. He looked fantastic. Clean, anxious. "I'm just glad to get you out of there. I have been worried sick about you Celeste. It's been some long days for all of us."

"Thank you Marvin. Thank you so much. How did you get here?" Celeste asked wondering if there was a rental car.

"I took a cab. You want to go to the airport now?" He asked.

"No, my rental car was left in Metairie. We should go get it. You flew into New Orleans?" Celeste was surprised, when she had tried that option did not look good.

"Yeah, and there is a flight out of here too. Let's get a cab then and go get the car." Marvin began walking her to a cab parked on the street.

When they pulled up to the rental car, they found the trunk open. Marvin asked the cab to wait a minute and they both got out of the car. The tent and supplies were gone. Celeste was going to leave them for someone who could use them once she was heading back to Oregon anyway. It looked like that had already happened. Her personal belongings in the carry on were also gone, as were the tires on this rental car.

Celeste laughed a bit hysterically. "Well, fuck. Okay then. I can't even drive this bitch back to the rental company."

Celeste looked down the road that led to Laurent's home, fallen trees and pieces of wood, sheetrock and pipes blocked good passage of the road. It hurt to see this and she tried to look past all of it, but realizing Laurent was not there, and even if she could make it to his home knew she would not find him there.

Marvin led her back to the cab and they headed to the airport. He was shocked at the damage all around them. Celeste felt damaged herself. She had seen so much. Her need to see and experience had been fulfilled. She was over it.

They returned the keys to the car rental spot at the Louis Armstrong airport. Celeste tried to just tell them where the car was, and that a flatbed tow truck would be needed. They wanted paperwork filled out, so many questions answered and she just did not have that in her. After four days of sitting up barely sleeping, hearing awful stories and seeing awful things she was depleted and told them she simply could not fill out those papers.

Marvin came to her aid. "You have all of her contact information. You have the keys and the location of the car. This will have to be enough for today." He then he steered her out.

The fact that the keys were being returned to a different airport than rented from, the fact that the car was damaged and needed picked up, were just beyond her control right now. It would be handled, and her part in it dealt with another day. This day she had nothing left to give mentally, emotionally or physically.

Celeste had not brushed her teeth, combed her hair, or washed her face in four days. Had not been able to lie down, wash herself, change her clothes or eat anything other than a bologna sandwiches three times a day. She had a severe caffeine withdrawal headache. The stench of jail and the ordeal clung to her. Her nerves were absolutely shot.

Marvin took her to get an espresso and then they searched for food. There was two hours until they boarded for the flight home.

They enjoyed a meal that seemed to Celeste, like food for royalty. It was at Zatarains, and Celeste could honestly say this was the high light of her trip.

Once on the plane, Celeste cried. Gut wrenching, but quietly. She knew she would need to process what she had just endured. She could not wait to get home, shower every inch of herself with suds, and lay down on her firm bed with its clean sheets. Marvin held her and she fell asleep as they flew across country...

*****

Celeste's story will continue.

Authors note:

By 2006 there were over five hundred unidentified bodies still not named, as money ran out and efforts lost steam.

The ninth ward was hit the hardest and curfew would be in place for a very long time after. Tens of thousands of black working class people, one year later would still not be able to return. Heaps of rubble, debris, dead dogs and rats would still be present. Some schools, still having no place to meet...

There was still no electricity in many sections of the city. Even year's later, New Orleans had the highest murder rate in the country, and some say the only profitable business was the drug trade. A lot of Hispanics came in and lived in substandard conditions to rebuild the city, but so much more needed to be done.

So many victims and so much loss.

Wind and water were very powerful elements of nature. When combined with the fury released with Katrina, the damage was unbelievable and unimaginable until it does happen for real.

## Big Mama's Praline

2 cups sugar

1/8 teaspoon salt

1 teaspoon baking soda

2 Tablespoons butter

1 cup buttermilk

2 1/1 cups pecans

Use a heavy saucepan and combine all ingredients except the pecans. Cook over high heat for 5 minutes; stir constantly until candy reaches the softball stage (approximately 5 minutes).Remove from heat and let cool slightly. Then stir in pecans and beat until light and creamy. Drop from tablespoon onto wax paper and let cool.

Big Mama said: "don't even bother to try and make candy when it rains." Well, I have made these candies many times and sometimes they are so perfect, beautiful and delicious and other times just don't do right, so I will go with what she says and don't even bother when it is rainy.

Bon Appetit Chere

CPSIA information can be obtained
at www.ICGtesting.com
Printed in the USA
LVHW081840140822
725923LV00008B/540

9 781519 158949